PRAISE FOR ALLA CRONE'S BOOKS

EAST LIES THE SUN

Gold Medal winner of West Coast Review of Books

"… was an immediate success…an exciting book…historically accurate"
(Santa Rosa Press Democrat)

"Alla Crone's byline will be eagerly sought by readers … the book brims with the authentic flavor of the time"
(Sonoma Index Tribune)

RODINA

Alla Crone has a gift for creating a sense of place, whether it is Shanghai during the bombing of 1937, or San Francisco in 1947…The author also creates the ominous atmosphere of the Cold War. The historical crisis intensifies her (the heroine's) own dilemma as a woman without a country. There are stormy passions here… Vickie is a survivor and a kind of role model for women who want wholeness and harmony…
(The Press Democrat)

WINDS OVER MANCHURIA

"is written with the style and tradition of Ayn Rand"
(Book Reviews, L'Affaire de Coeur)

LEGACY OF AMBER

Alla Crone successfully blended the political, cultural and romantic themes making her story work on all levels."
(Publishers Weekly)

NORTH OF THE MOON

"Three novels about history, culture and romance…have propelled Alla Crone into national attention …North of the Moon captures the sweep and passion of the period and the authenticity is remarkable."
(San Mateo Times)

Also by Alla Crone

East Lies the Sun
Winds Over Manchuria
North Of the Moon
Legacy of Amber
Rodina
Maxim

The Other Side of Life

Alla Crone

my best wishes,
Alla Crone

authorHOUSE®

AuthorHouse™
1663 Liberty Drive
Bloomington, IN 47403
www.authorhouse.com
Phone: 1-800-839-8640

First published by AuthorHouse 2/23/2011

ISBN: 978-1-4567-2726-0 (e)
ISBN: 978-1-4567-2724-6 (dj)
ISBN: 978-1-4567-2723-9 (sc)

Library of Congress Control Number: 2011900611

Printed in the United States of America

To Vicka Surovtsov, my friend of many lives…

My doctrine is: Live that thou mayest desire to live again, – that is thy duty, – for in any case thou will live again!

(Friedrich Nietzsche)

CHAPTER 1

1982

At first glance everything looked the same. The French Provincial Furniture, the white bedspreads, the matching plush carpeting. Yet something looked different and I was confused.

Seconds earlier the morning sun had been flooding the guestroom, its light blinding, its heat uncomfortable.

Now twilight surrounded me, dim and shadowy. I rubbed my forehead. "What the hell?"

I glanced out the window. The bright blue sky of a moment ago had turned the color of a tarnished steel plate. It hung low over the golf course. Blurred shapes moved on the grass—darted, zigzagged, paused. Golfers, I thought. But no. They wouldn't all be dressed in the same gray clothing, monochromatic and dull. The whole landscape appeared dull, and the clubhouse, perched on a distant knoll, was obscured by rolling, churning fog. I heard no voices, and had trouble seeing.

The guestroom where I stood looked dark and hazy. I had difficulty discerning familiar objects. The red needlepoint pillows embroidered by my wife's mother years ago in Germany, lay neatly on the bedspreads, but the cuckoo clock with its carved wood antlers hanging on the right wall not four feet away was barely visible through an almost black shadow. Its ticking sounded hollow.

Where had the day gone? I tried to mentally retrace my steps. Only a few minutes ago, I came into the guestroom to get my coat out of the spare closet. I was about to leave the house for the hospital, to make rounds and then scrub for surgery. I shook my head. What's going on?

My glance wandered to the foot of the bed and stopped there. I sensed that what lay beyond the bed would give me the answers, yet I dreaded those answers. Still, my curiosity got the better of me, and driven by some outside force, I looked down. There, through the dark haze, I could distinguish a shapeless form. The blood seemed to rise to my eyes, half-blinding me.

I moved closer.

A body lay at my feet. One leg, grotesquely twisted, peered from under the torso on one side. The right hand clutched the tassels of the bedspread. I bent over for a closer look and found myself staring into the unseeing eyes of my own face.

"My God!"

I took a shaky step backward, my heart leaping to my throat. Fragmented thoughts, like painful particles of hot sand, needled my brain, making me wince. A thought flashed through my mind, something Gretchen had said. My wife,who was born and raised in Frankfurt, studied metaphysics with her mother's friend who exerted great influence on Gretchen's young mind. I tried to remember what she had said to me about death when I came home one day distressed about losing one of my patients.

"When you're deprived of a physical body," she had said to me then, taking both my hands into hers, "your emotions vibrate at a higher rate of frequency. Both the good and the bad are intensified. You say that your patient was a good man, so he would be happy now."

She let go of my hands and kissed me, but I shook my head, dismissing her words as so much nonsense.

Now, I examined my hands, expecting to see through them, but to my relief, they were solid. I pinched my forearm and the resulting pain was comforting. Nothing had changed in my body and I could still control my movements.

Relieved, I wanted to sit down and think how to make myself wake up from this nightmare. Gretchen's favorite Louis XV chair stood nearby. It rested under the small writing desk and I reached to pull it out. It didn't move. My hand, firm to my own touch, went right through it. I tried again. Nothing. Panic seized me. Frantically, I tried to grasp the chair, its dainty silk covered arms, its seat, but my hand clutched at the air instead. I swore and pounded my fist into the palm of the other hand. The sound of my own voice startled me.

I had no wounds, felt no pain, and was in control of all my faculties. Then it dawned on me that the low-back pain I had developed over the last five years was gone. I even experienced a sense of euphoric lightness in my body, which I had not known since the days when I was thirty pounds lighter and twenty years younger.

A full-length mirror in a gold frame hung beside one of the twin beds. At the time Gretchen hung it, I objected to its location. "It's too suggestive," I grumbled, my strict Catholic upbringing rising to the fore. Gretchen laughed. "Oh, don't be such a prig," she had said, tossing her copper hair off her forehead and straightening the mirror. "Let our house-guests enjoy themselves." She winked at me provocatively. "Watching yourself during sex can be very exciting."

I remember flushing with embarrassment, but now I rushed toward it, expecting to look at my ruddy face and six-foot frame, but instead, a dim reflection of the opposite wall with its cross-stitched hanging stared back at me. I must have overstepped the range of vision. When I moved sideways I suddenly became aware of an object enveloping my right ankle.

I glanced down and recoiled. My foot had gone through the body's head on the floor. *My* head? I jerked back and forced myself to look in the mirror again. Nothing. Not even a trace of my outline in the twilight. In one leap I found myself in front of the mirror, both hands reaching out to the frame, so that no optical error could trick me. But my hands couldn't make contact with it, and I still stared at the reflection of the opposite wall.

All the buoyancy I felt a moment ago drained out of me. I dropped my hands. That heap on the floor... "God! How can it be? I'm not dead. Surely I'm *not dead!*"

I headed for the door. With my hand on the knob, I stopped and tensed. I had read stories of ghosts condemned to haunt areas of their deaths for centuries. But I was not a ghost and I was *not dead.* I could still think, feel, and I was made of solid matter.

I grasped the knob only to have my empty fist tremble when the nails bore into the palm of my hand. Helpless to open the door, I hoped my cries could be heard in the house. Steve had driven off to school early in the morning, and it was not Mrs. Swanson's cleaning day. But Gretchen was home.

"Gretchen!" I called. No response. I shouted, I hit the door with an open palm. It took only a few seconds for me to realize that with each thrust of my arm, the momentum had carried it *through* the door. I stared at my hand when it penetrated the door and disappeared behind it. I only saw the stump of my wrist on my side of the door. I pulled my arm back and my hand reappeared. Damn! I inched closer. When my face reached the panel, I stopped. Hell, there was something demeaning in the thought that I, Dr. James Braddock, had suddenly become an ethereal entity unable to open doors. Still, I closed my eyes and pushed forward with my entire body. When I opened my eyes, I found myself in the hallway leading to the living room. I turned around. The door to the guestroom was closed. I had gone through it without feeling any contact with physical objects. I had become a ghost to the physical world.

I took a few shaky steps down the hall with a nagging feeling of unfinished business. I have always thought myself a pragmatist, a man of methodical logic, but at this moment my mind went out of control. As I reached my study, a muffled moan reached me from the guestroom. I froze. That sound, like an invisible magnet, began to pull me back into the guestroom, but this time through an opened door. Did Gretchen open it while I entered the study?

That moan. Maybe I survived after all. Yet, I resisted the strong pull toward the body on the floor. Then I heard another sound. Far away. So far I barely recognized it – the siren of an approaching ambulance.

I turned toward the door. But before I could reach it, total blackness enveloped me.

* * *

"Code Blue! Code Blue!"

The hospital staff of St.Anthony's Hospital in San Francisco was used to such a summons, but I detected an odd urgency in the announcer's voice. The nurses, running down the hall behind the crash cart, looked at each other with worried frowns. They found pandemonium inside the emergency room. The patient was on a gurney receiving CPR, while technicians were busy hooking up various color-coded tubes that lead from the CC module to the patient -- green for oxygen, white for suction, and a big red one for the ventilator. A rectangular pillar, like a monolith, the module stood out of the way so that everyone could see the display monitor on top.. The nurses positioned the crash cart beside the gurney, and the emergency team

went to work on the inert patient. A few moments later, the door
to the emergency room flew open and Doctors Bob Rice and Sam
Weaver rushed in.

"Who is it?" barked Sam, looking down at the patient. "Oh, my
God, it's Jim Braddock! What happened?"

One of the nurses answered. "The medics said Dr.Braddock's
wife called 911 and when they got there, they found him lying on the
bedroom floor in cardiac arrest."

"What was his rhythm when you guys hooked him up to the
monitor?" Sam Weaver asked.

"V-fib."

"Did you shock him?"

"Yes, doctor."

"How much did you give him?"

"200, 300 and then 360 joules."

"And?"

"Nothing."

"Well, he's getting good CPR. What drugs have you given him
up to this point?"

1 amp of EPI."

"What happened then?"

"Nothing, so we popped him again with 360 joules."

"OK. Let's give him another amp of EPI."

The nurse promptly pushed in the rhythm-stimulating drug.

""What are we seeing up there now?"

"V-Tach, no pulse."

"Damn! Let's go ahead and buzz him with 360 joules."

"OK! Everybody clear?"

ZAP! The body jerked from the shock and then fell back on the
gurney inert.

"Didn't work. Do it again about 360 joules."

ZAP!

"We have a rhythm. Any blood pressure?"

"No."

"Then keep massaging and let's go ahead and try Lidocaine IV."

Both physicians watched in silence while the nurses carried out this order. Then Bob Rice said, "Great. Any blood pressure?"

"We got a little bit."

"OK. Keep working."

"Now he's got a better rhythm and blood pressure."

"Let's back off on the massage. Oh shit! There he goes!"

"Any blood pressure?"

"No."

"Resume CPR."

*   *   *

"The joke is on me," I thought, watching from a corner of the room while my inert body was being worked on. "Those near-death stories my patients told me...which I disdained.... what the hell! It must be happening to me. I yell and Sam can't hear me. So, am I dead or what?"

Frantic for any human contact, I shouted at the nurses, at Sam and Bob, but the staff ignored me. In my fury, my sight blurred, I moved away trying to obliterate the scene.

To calm myself, I tried to reconstruct the details of the day but couldn't remember what brought on my heart attack. As I thought about it intently, I suddenly found myself back in my home.

Once inside my study however, I knew that I couldn't make anything move. Gretchen, no doubt, was at the hospital, and Steve was in school. Gretchen! Oh God, now I remembered! We had a fight at breakfast this morning, one of those bitter arguments we've been having lately over Steve, and the higher she raised her voice, the higher my blood pressure rose. Furious at her for taking sides with Steve, frustrated at my inability to make her see my side of the argument, I remember storming out of the kitchen and slamming the guestroom door before heading for the closet.

But now, in my study, I went to my desk, a large Danish modern that Gretchen and I had purchased in Europe. It was strewn with papers and unpaid bills I intended to clear up this weekend. I tried to pick up the top envelope. My hand went through it and disappeared underneath.

Then it came to me what I needed to do. The insurance on my son's car. A few days ago I was searching for one of my medical articles and had pushed a stack of bills to one side, leaving them unattended until this morning when I discovered that the car insurance had expired. I had intended to write a check then and there, but Gretchen called me in for breakfast and I left the checkbook on the desk planning to take care of the bill before leaving the house.

Steve was driving around in an uninsured car. He might be in an accident and hurt himself or someone else. I shuddered. The checkbook lay nearby and I tried again and again to grasp it. What about telekinesis? Gretchen had told me that by applied concentration of will it can be possible to lift small objects off the table. My reaction to her words had been, "What nonsense!" But now, desperate, I stared at the stack of papers. I could see the corner of the insurance bill under two or three other envelopes. I sighed in relief. It shouldn't be too hard to lift off the top layers. But how to apply my will? The only way I could think of was to visualize them lifting and moving. To do that, I needed to concentrate, to direct my thought solely on the task. But that seemed impossible. I was caught in a whirlpool of emotions.

I was afraid to try. What if I failed? Maybe I should wait until my anxiety subsided. I walked over to the window, turned around, paced the room, then stopped at the desk. Shaking all over, I closed my eyes and concentrated on the papers. I didn't know how long I stood there. Time seemed to have lost all meaning–before I opened my eyes and looked down. Nothing happened. The papers lay exactly where they were when I first found them. I tried again and again without success.

When I paused to think of a new approach–the insurance bill taunting me from under the letters so near to my hand and so completely inaccessible–my glance fell on the checkbook again. I felt weak in my knees. My attempts at telekinesis were futile. Even if I had been successful in moving the papers to the side, I still couldn't write a check, tear it off the stub, enclose it in the envelope and seal it. Gretchen had called it an out-of-body experience. So, physical world with its simple, everyday gestures was totally beyond my reach. How I wished now that I had listened to her gentle revelations about the shadowy world on the other side of life which I was facing now. So many times I would cut her off in mid-sentence, causing a painful look and a single tear to sneak out of her eye.

The suspense of whether my colleagues were going to succeed or fail in reviving me was more than I could bear. Hitting my fist into the palm of my hand, I swore. I felt like kicking my desk chair but even that dubious privilege was denied me. I began to see a glimmer of humor in my situation, and the words of Charles Farnsworth, my former professor of anatomy in medical school came back to me, "When all else fails, hitting your head against the wall is not going to improve things." He would hit the top of his desk with his fist for emphasis and add forcefully, "Think again." Tall and angular with graying wavy hair, his transparent gray eyes saw right through us as if he were reading the innermost secrets of our souls. With a thin punctuated laugh, a chuckle really, he would dissect the problem and solve it with a precise economy of words. It was rumored that he dabbled in metaphysics, but in those days I had no interest in such esoteric matters.

I wondered what had brought the professor to my mind, a man I had not thought of in years. With a sigh, I turned to the checkbook on the desk and tried again and again to grasp it.

"Is this hell?" I cried out in frustration.

"No, Jim, just ignorance."

I recognized the voice instantly. Shaken, I wheeled around and stared in shock.

Silhouetted against a bright white light, Dr. Farnsworth who had been dead for ten years, stood smiling at me. In spite of the haze and darkness that surrounded me I could see the professor clearly. His eyes were luminous and more penetrating than I remembered. He did not look through me. *He saw me.*

"My God, professor, am I--am I really dead?" I coughed to cover up the tremor in my voice. As I waited for his answer, I recalled the wry humor, the sharp double rap of the pointer he used to call his obstreperous students to attention. While weighing a particularly prickly question, he would ruffle his graying hair behind his left ear, and now, I watched my teacher pondering my question in much the same manner.

After a long pause, the professor said, "What is death, Jim? Do I seem dead to you?"

"Of course not, but—but—" I stumbled over words, fully aware that he had died ten years earlier.

Dr. Farnsworth held out his hand but I took a step back. What if my hand went through the professor's and we couldn't make contact? I wanted to maintain the illusion that at last I could communicate with someone normally.

"Don't be afraid, Jim," Dr. Farnsworth said. He took a step toward me and when I still hesitated, he added, "Come on, give me your hand."

Reluctantly I reached out, but before I could make myself touch him, Dr. Farnsworth grabbed my hand and shook it firmly. His flesh felt warm and comforting, and it broke down the wall between illusion and reality I'd been erecting so carefully. I lunged toward him, grasped his shoulders and shook him to convince myself that he was indeed of solid matter. I touched his hair, his face, his hands. Satisfied at last, I stifled a sob.

Dr. Farnsworth put his arm around my shoulders and for a brief moment a great calm enveloped me. Like a small boy who finds security in his father's embrace, I clutched his arm and refused to let go of it.

"All right, Jim, pull yourself together. I know it's harder to do on this side of life, but try just the same."

When I released the arm, he nodded. "That's better. Come on, follow me."

"Where?"

"I'm taking you away from your house," he said firmly.

I panicked. "Why?"

"Patience, Jim. Remember my classes? Dissect a small piece of tissue at a time. The same holds true over here."

At the front door, I paused and touched the professor's sleeve. He wore one of the gray tweed sport coats which he'd once favored in the classroom and its rough texture gave me added reassurance.

"Professor, nothing is the way I thought it would be," I blurted out. "I read somewhere that a person is supposed to have a restful sleep after —after—" I couldn't bring myself to say the word, for I felt very much alive.

"Normally, that's the case after a long illness," the professor said, "but yours was a sudden heart attack with an unknown outcome. Your friends are still working on you in that emergency room doing everything they can to bring you back to life." He smiled. "Do come along."

I started to follow him, and then stopped. "They're not supermen, Professor. They can work on me just so long before they give up. I can't stay here, I have to go back."

"What appears to be a long time on this side, has really been only a minute or so on the physical plane. Let's go."

Outside our gate, Professor Farnsworth stopped and turned to face me. "I want you to do exactly as I tell you. Close your eyes and repeat to yourself that you want to follow me wherever I go. Now, do it."

Although terrified of the unknown, I followed his instructions, and after what seemed only a second or two, the professor said, "You may look, Jim."

I don't know what I expected to see or whether I had even time to think about it, but nothing had prepared me for the scene before me.

We were standing in the middle of the most luxuriant valley I have ever seen. Rolling hills on both sides sparkled with a profusion of field flowers – orange, yellow, white, lavender. Verdant orchards hugged the hills and here and there liquidambar trees nodded lazily in the gentle breeze. The sun and the sky dazzled the eye. I stood taking in the shimmering landscape where the air was filled with a symphony of sounds so exquisite that my whole being thrilled in response. My body felt light, suspended in space, buoyed by the serenity around me.

The professor's voice broke into my euphoria. "Well, how does it feel to have the haze gone?"

"What happened to it, Dr. Farnsworth? Where are we?"

"Until this moment you've been seeing the physical world. Since it's in another dimension, it appeared hazy and dark to you, but now you are seeing a landscape in the higher energy field."

It was a relief to discover that I was not floating on clouds dressed in white robes, and that I stood on firm ground much as I would in the physical world. I shook my head in wonder. "I must say, this is more beautiful than anything I've ever seen on earth."

"Don't say 'earth'. What you really mean is the physical world. You haven't gone anywhere. Do you honestly think that we are somewhere in space or on another planet?"

"Aren't we?"

Professor Farnsworth laughed. "No! We're right where we've always been. The only difference is that we're in another dimension. The higher energy plane and the physical plane interpenetrate without interfering with each other's functions. And you're right. It *is* more beautiful here. You'll understand why later."

"I've never seen anything so serene, so peaceful."

Professor Farnsworth studied my face in silence for a while, and then said, "I wish you could stay here forever, Jim, but you can't." He gave me a compassionate look. "Don't forget, they're working on you in the hospital. In the meantime, try to get hold of yourself."

As I looked at him now standing beside me with the lush landscape spread at our feet, the professor scratched behind his ear again and I had the uncanny feeling that nothing had really changed since my student days and Dr. Farnsworth was still my mentor and teacher. I could see the professor in the classroom clearly, as if the twenty years had not blurred the picture. He never sat at his desk but sauntered across the classroom delivering his lectures on anatomy, describing the intricacies of the pectoralis major muscle or the tendons of the upper arm with affection of a master craftsman. He wove a tapestry of logic so simple that memorizing anatomical nomenclature became an exercise in rhythmic sounds, a trick we students used successfully in other fields of our study.

I sank on the soft fresh grass and with a sigh leaned against a tree. Restless, I couldn't relax. What about my loved ones still in the physical world?

The professor placed his hand on my arm. "Rest, Jim. There's time."

His touch was so reassuring that I choked up and was only able to nod.

Suddenly, a brilliant light appeared nearby. I saw an outline of a woman bathed in a golden halo but could not see her face. An all-consuming love filled my whole being. I was drawn to her, I wanted to know who she was, yet somehow I already knew that she was someone I loved for a long time. My urge to touch her was so overwhelming that I jumped up and with outstretched arms rushed toward her, but the light melted away and she was gone before I could reach her.

"Who is she, Professor?" I asked turning around, but he was gone too. I closed my eyes trying to recreate the dazzling vision but it eluded me. I retraced my steps to the tree and sliding down, leaned against it again. I didn't even know her name, yet I loved her. Somewhere. Some time. In another life? My thoughts turned to Gretchen who believed in reincarnation and often repeated that we lived more than once. I was an agnostic and always dismissed her attempts to convince me as flights of fancy.

And now? How could I logically explain my spontaneous reaction to the vision of a woman whose face I couldn't even see? I yearned to see her again, to touch her and find out who she was. Frustrated, I sighed and tried to calm myself. No luck. A sudden breeze feathered my forehead, then dashed on to agitate the leaves of a nearby maple tree.

No answers came.

CHAPTER 2

I must have dozed off, because when I opened my eyes, I gasped. "Mother!"

She took a step toward me and put her hands out. I embraced her and held her close for the first time in twenty years.

"Oh, Jim, it's *so* good to have you *see* me."

She still had that peculiarity of speech where she underscored certain words for emphasis.

I pushed her away and held her at arm's length, swallowing tears and struggling to find my voice.

"Mother, what a strange greeting. Why didn't you say 'it's so good to *see* you?"

She smiled and nodded, another familiar gesture she had carried over. "Ah, but I've been seeing *you* all along."

I studied her closely. Dressed in a Scotch plaid Pendleton skirt and a blue pullover, she looked like she did in her thirties, her light brown hair short and curly, her hazel eyes twinkling with mirth, her face glowing with health.

She held my face between the palms of her hands. "You are still handsome, Jim, but a little tired."

Her sweet voice with just a suggestion of a nasal twang, made me feel so carefree that I hugged her, lifting her off the ground.

"Jim, let me go, you make me dizzy."

I put her down gently, happy to see her alive.

In fact, the whole area where we stood vibrated with blinding brilliance. Trees, flowers, the very ground we stood on were so sharply delineated that it made me think of a bold and brightly colored painting.

As if she were reading my thoughts, Mother said, "Jim, don't be afraid. I won't disappear. At least not while you are in your out-of-body state. We are in the same dimension while you're in the emergency room."

I didn't want to think about that.

Childhood memories loosened and came flooding back, both a reminder of my adolescent days and a gentle reproach to my selfishness. I dominated her life, taking for granted that I was the center of it, especially after my father died suddenly from a heart attack when I was only eight year old. He had been a struggling architect and left a small life insurance, which, coupled with my mother's bookkeeping job, allowed us to live modestly and free from debts. I missed him deeply and clung to my mother, terrified that I might lose her too. So, when Jack Spencer, the local pharmacist, appeared on the scene a few years after my father died, I became jealous immediately, and took an instant dislike to him.

Perhaps it was that strange new smile that crossed my mother's face whenever she talked about Jack that threatened my world –I don't know –but I became sullen and difficult. I adored her and couldn't cope with the thought of sharing her with another man.

No words were ever spoken between us about Jack but my hurt and disappointed looks had not escaped my mother who had asked me several times if anything was the matter. When I said 'nothing', she let it go at that.

Before long, however, she stopped seeing Jack and we resumed our quiet life in the Sonoma County north of San Francisco. We lived in a two-bedroom house with a wrap-around porch on the outskirts of the town of Santa Rosa. In retrospect I should have been happy that we lived comfortably without debts and had food on the table every night. But in my adolescence I saw our small house and garden an embarrassment next to big mansions at the end of our street. Mercedes and Cadillacs floated past me while I sat on the steps of our porch leafing through a sports magazine and waiting for Mother to come home from work. I saw uniformed kids in the back of those cars being driven home from their private schools and fantasized that I was one of them. I squirmed at the sight of rusted pieces of metal from a dented fender that permanently occupied a portion of the neighbor's yard and I vowed that when I grew up, I would get a well-paying profession and earn a good enough living to own a larger home in a neat neighborhood.

I worked hard during my school years and shared all my achievements and failures with my mother. She followed my studies, listened not only with patience but with genuine interest to my explanations of various laboratory experiments, and I knew she understood them because she would interrupt me occasionally, ask probing questions, clap her hands in delight when she understood and frankly apologize when it went over her head.

In my last year of medical school, I noticed that Mother looked pale and tired easily. I urged her to see our family physician but she waved me away.

"You like to play doctor, don't you, Jim? There's nothing wrong with me. I've been overdoing it at the office and need to take a break."

"When was the last time you had a physical, Mom? If you don't make an appointment, I will."

She had her physical that showed leukemia in advanced stages. She accepted it long before I did and had all her affairs in order before the end approached. I couldn't face the inevitable. I took time off from school to care for her, hoping for a remission that would give us time to find a new cure. I wept when she died, bitter to be left without either parent at the age of 25. I took out a loan and plunged deep into my training to drown my grief.

Now, seeing my mother after so many years, I realized that I had kept her from having a life of her own. After my father's death, she had still been young and charming and had deserved personal happiness. The past congealed with the present and I sighed. "I guess I was a bit of a pill, wasn't I, Mom?" I said.

"What do you mean?"

"I mean my attitude toward Jack."

"It wasn't in my plan to cross over here so soon. I waited for you to finish school and then planned to let loose and make a new life for myself." Mother winked at me and shook her finger. "Don't attach so much importance to yourself, dear."

"I can hardly do it over here," I said lowering myself heavily on the velvety grass. "I have become a non-entity." I hesitated, studying her face. "I'm ashamed of what I've failed to do with my life. How little we know ourselves. And here, I don't know how to cope."

"Why not doze a little, and see what happens when you wake up."

"I don't want to sleep. I'd like to go back to my house. You're telling me to distance myself from the only thing that makes me feel that I'm still Jim Braddock. This place here"–I waved my hand around the spectacular landscape–"is foreign to me, beautiful, but foreign just the same. I want to be in my home where everything is familiar and where I can be in control!"

As soon as I said it, I realized how foolish it must have sounded to my mother. I shifted on the grass and laughed. "What a pompous ass I am!"

Mother came up to me and patted my head the way she used to

do when I was a youngster. "That you are, my dear, but in spite of it, I'm on *your* side. I advise you never to go back to your house. In this dimension all you have to do is to think strongly of a place you want to be and you will be there instantly. But there are good reasons for you not to go back. If you don't sever your ties to your house now, it'll be more difficult for you later if your friends in the emergency room fail to revive you."

I jumped up and began to pace. "Mom, for heaven's sake, I need to take stock of what's happening to me. What harm is there in my going home instead of staying here?"

Mother was relentless. "The harm is in your denial of what's happening to you. I'm trying to prepare you for the possibility that you may not be revived down there. Promise me that you will not return to your house."

I couldn't believe how difficult I found it to give such a promise. "I'll do my best, Mother," I muttered without conviction. But I knew she had a point and I behaved like a stubborn child.

She took my hand. "Jim, I'm going away now but I'll be watching over you. Remember, you'll never be alone even if you *think* and *feel* alone."

Moments later, she was gone. I sank wearily onto the grass again, trying to relax, but the thoughts about my home and family wouldn't leave me. I loved our comfortable, U-shaped house with a swimming pool in the back. Along the edges of the pool I had planted my favorite pink and white petunias. I loved puttering in the garden — it gave me release from pressures of my surgical practice and the area was small enough to be a pleasure instead of a burden. Clumps of yellow and purple pansies in the four corners of the cement walkway around the pool needed pruning. I intended to do that over the weekend with Steve's help. He too, loved gardening. Gretchen often wanted me to go to the movies with her, but she usually picked some silly romantic comedy and I preferred to work in our garden and would tell her to go with a girlfriend instead.

"Then why don't *you* pick a movie you'd like to see?" she said one afternoon while Steve and I were on our knees weeding a flower bed.

"The garden needs work, Gretchen. Can't you see that Steve and I are busy here?" I couldn't keep annoyance out of my voice.

Gretchen turned and ran toward the house but not before raising her voice at me, "I'm only trying to make you forget your stressful work for a couple of hours, so you can relax completely. I bet you're still thinking of your patients while you do the gardening."

*   *   *

How I wished now that I could turn the clock back and be aware of her needs as well, be willing to spend more time with her, be more considerate and loving.

I thought of all the things I put off, planning to get to them this weekend. Now they were out of reach. It was unrealistic to expect Gretchen to take care of the garden now – she didn't know how. Steve, cheerful and obliging, would have to take over and try to fill in for me where he could. But he was only seventeen. I felt a rush of guilt. I left him so abruptly and without guidance. Aside from gardening, I had spent so little time with my son throughout his formative years. There were always other priorities. Backlog of paperwork, overflow of outpatients, scheduled surgeries.

Steve. I ached to see him. We had been close during those rare times when I could give him my attention. How I regretted now that those were indeed rare times. I was always off to yet another emergency surgery or a staff meeting and when he needed me most, I wasn't there.

Belatedly I realized now that he had yearned for my company

and wanted to share with me his joys and disappointments but I had failed to see this need and devoted more time to the narrow circle of my medical world. The argument with Gretchen this morning was the case in point. Steve's science grades were poor and he had confided to his mother that he wanted to give up the idea of going to medical school. Instead, he wanted to pursue a career in graphic art. Gretchen told me about it over breakfast and defended his wish. Steve had shown no indication that he didn't want to follow in my footsteps until his grades began to slip. When Gretchen took his side, all my arguments were wasted. She screamed at me the final insult, "You want Steve to become a reluctant physician just so he can follow in your footsteps. I know how much you love your work, and I really try to be supportive. I know the pressures you are under, but Steve's heart isn't in it! It would flatter your ego to say your son is a doctor too!"

Triggered by this last remark, my anger spiraled out of control. "That's not fair!" I yelled back, "I want Steve to have a respectable profession and a lucrative career. What can he do with .graphic art? He has never shown any talent in that direction. He's just too lazy to apply himself and improve his grades."

I stormed out of the kitchen, rushed to the guestroom to get my coat, and slammed the door behind me.

That was the last I remembered.

I wanted to hug Steve now, to listen to his arguments, and then to turn back the clock to those days when I had given him some time playing catch or listening to his childish chatter, watching his freckled face glowing with enthusiasm. He was a good boy, cheerful, frisky and loving. When he was born, I thought myself the happiest, the most blessed man on earth. And in spite of everything that had happened, I had to admit that Gretchen was a good mother. She adored Steve, yet she was strict, influenced by her own mother with whom she kept in close touch through frequent correspondence and periodic overseas phone calls.

*   *   *

I could never forget the first time I had met her mother. It happened shortly after Gretchen had been hired as a secretary in our Army offices in Frankfurt where I had been assigned after joining the service. Gretchen invited me to visit her home and her invitation came as a mild surprise, for we had only known each other for a few days. Nevertheless, I accepted eagerly. Here was an opportunity for me to get into a private home and see how people of another country lived. Besides, Gretchen attracted me with her vivacious personality, her spontaneity and provocative smile.

In my youth I had not traveled abroad and an army career seemed to offer an ideal opportunity to see the world and learn about other peoples. My mother worked hard to make ends meet after my father died, so there was never any question about travel while I was in school. Years later, when my overseas assignment came through for Germany, I was thrilled and studied the country's map and history.

In extending her invitation, Gretchen told me that she and her mother lived modestly since her father had died two years earlier, a broken man who had seen his machine parts factory destroyed by arson, and who had never recovered from the shock of losing in a few seconds his carefully nurtured and prosperous business. Gretchen could never forget how he had staggered home covered with ashes, his eyes wild, his clothing torn, screaming profanity at no one in particular.

From that day on he lived withdrawn into a secretive world of his own, sealed in the cocoon of the past and rejecting the present with the singular cunning of those whose emotional trauma remains unresolved.

In the vain hope that a change of environment might bring him back to reality, Gretchen's mother sold their large home and rented a two bedroom apartment in a less affluent area. But he soon died leaving them with some mementoes of old wealth, much pride, and little else. Gretchen's hope for a college degree had to be abandoned, and after she finished high school, she took a short business course and went to work as a clerk-typist.

I could see that Gretchen was defensive in describing her reduced circumstances, and I told her that people themselves interested me and not where they lived.

I found the address with difficulty because my college German had become rusty and I had trouble with the street signs. When I entered, her mother received me imperiously from a hard straight-back chair. I felt awkward in her presence, tempted toward a theatrical obeisance. Her wispy graying hair was pulled back in a small bun on the top of her head and pinned with two long hairpins. Dressed in a high-necked gray dress trimmed with crocheted lace, she kept her hands folded on her lap while scrutinizing me with her watery eyes. Her long face with a pointed chin bore no trace of a smile when I gave her a bouquet of flowers and according to European custom, kissed her hand. She took the flowers and handed them to Gretchen, then thanked me in passable English.

The place was cluttered with pieces of old furniture. A tapestry cloth covered the dining room table that dominated the center of the room and a baby grand piano was pushed into one corner, its top full of magazines, sheet music, and a cluster of family pictures.

Gretchen's mother questioned my background with interest and tact and I soon forgot her aloof manner. At the discovery that I was an only child like Gretchen, Frau Schneider succumbed to a conspiratorial smile and said in careful English, "The more siblings there are, the more quarrels there can be, ja?"

When I told her that I was planning on making the army my career, she approved. "You will travel abroad and serve your country at the same time," she concluded as she poured me tea into a delicately painted china cup and offered a dish of mouth-watering chocolate and cream-filled petit fours.

By the time I left an hour later, Frau Schneider's icy demeanor had melted into a motherly smile, her veined and arthritic hand constantly pushing the plate of cakes toward me, urging me between sentences to try just one more. I left their place shaken by the realization of how much I've missed the homey atmosphere of my mother's apartment and an older woman's warmth. All the years since my mother's death, I suppressed my emotions and wouldn't allow myself to dwell on the loving relationship that I had with her. For the first time since her death, tears welled up in my eyes and flowed down my cheeks while I drove back to my bachelor army quarters.

From that day on, I spent many evenings in Gretchen's apartment where Frau Schneider always greeted me with a welcoming smile, her imperious manner gradually melting away. A few minutes after my arrival, she would tactfully find an excuse to leave the room and go to the kitchen so Gretchen and I could be alone. Before long, I was hopelessly smitten by Gretchen, her copper hair unruly around her face, catching gold highlights in the sun, her sometimes shy, sometimes provocative smile sending messages to me better than any words could convey. There were other women in my life before her but they were fleeting involvements and I forgot them soon after each affair ended. But not with Gretchen. A kittenish look in her eyes, an inviting mouth with half-opened pink lips, and I was lost.

*   *   *

We started to spend a lot of time together during the week and on weekends. I often drove her to Heidelberg, the medieval college town on the banks of the Neckar River, only an hour's drive south. Its cone-shaped red roofs, geranium-studded balconies and needle-thin church steeples clustered in a narrow valley and hugged the hills below the ruins of a princely castle. The home of the old university, the town was sprinkled with student taverns, whose customers carried their lusty songs out into the misty air on the heady aroma of beer. White excursion boats alive with tourists and an accordionist–always an accordionist--playing lilting folk tunes, floated down the sparkling Neckar.

We climbed the hills for hours or walked the narrow *Hauptstrasse* stopping for a cup of coffee at an outdoor garden café. Over a piece of walnut torte with *schlagsahne* beneath the moving shade of blossoming chestnut trees, we discussed the merits of long hikes to which many Germans were addicted.

"You Americans behave like children," she once said with a twinkle in her eye.

"How's that?" I asked.

"Your cars are your cradles. You don't want to walk if you can drive. I've seen army wives drive two blocks between shops. More than that, the other day in the office, I overheard one wife tell another that she is trying to persuade her husband to buy her a car with an automatic transmission because it's too hard for her to drive a small Volkswagen with a clutch and manual shift. Soft life! How spoiled can you get?"

"It's easy to get used to creature comforts," I said, watching her take another piece of cake. "But don't be misled by what you call 'soft life'. Americans can be tough when necessary and persistent in pursuing our goals." I looked at her, pointedly sliding my gaze from her eyes to her small hands with tapered fingers. I took one of them into my hands, turned it over and kissed her palm. Surprisingly, she did not blush, only raised one brow and went on to delight in the walnut cake.

*   *   *

Her exuberance over mundane pleasures was a refreshing departure from the low-key reserve that I'd been used to at home. Several times we attended the theater near the old University and I enjoyed watching her when she applauded *Rosalinde* in *Die Fledermaus,* or swung in rhythm to the whirling tune of the *Merry Widow Waltz.* Occasionally I caught her look that fleeted past me like a hunted gazelle, a look which I thought was asking for approval, and inviting me to share in her joys. I grinned broadly in return, unable to understand the words sung in German and only vaguely pleased with the frothy music and the innocuous farce of the operetta.

Only once did I sense a touch of defensiveness in her voice when she spoke about her father.

She mesmerized me by her cat-like eyes, so familiar to me that had I not known her to be of foreign birth, I would have thought that we had met before. My thoughts were preoccupied with her during the day, and at night, when I dreamed about her, she always appeared to me wearing the same lemon yellow dress of the last century with her hair piled high on top of her head. Only in my dreams her hair was black and her slanted eyes brown instead of green.

Although I could not explain the significance of either the real or the imaginary Gretchen, I was fascinated by her whether she appeared before me as a brunette of the nineteenth century, dancing in a grand ballroom of some ornate palace, or as a flesh and blood redhead in my office. Spirited and joyful, she seemed to be drawn to me by an equally mysterious power.

Inevitably we married and although our courtship was short, I felt I had known her all my life.

I told her about my dreams and she turned pale. She put her arms on the table and leaned forward. "Describe the dress I'm wearing in your dreams," she said in an uncharacteristically anxious voice.

We were having an early dinner at one of the restaurants on the main *Hauptstrasse* in Heidelberg before driving back to Frankfurt. I looked at her curiously. In the flickering candlelight her short fluffed curls shone with copper highlights that effectively underscored the pallor of her skin. Unlike many redheads, she had dark brows framing her green eyes that now all but bore into me.

"I don't remember the details," I said, "but it is always a yellow dress with a low cut neckline trimmed in lace, long white gloves and lots of strands of pearls cascading down your bosom."

She shuddered. "It's spooky. It frightens me. Would you believe if I told you that I have similar dreams where I'm always dressed in that same yellow dress you describe? The only difference is that I never see myself dancing in a ballroom, and sometimes I'm dressed in a long black dress standing in a white columned gazebo in a beautiful park with a pond full of swans."

My heart flipped painfully in my chest, for her description caused a moment of deep melancholy that flashed by and vanished before I could grasp its meaning. I forced a smile. "Now I've learned something new about you." And when she looked at me with raised brows, I said, "You have an active imagination in linking our dreams."

She straightened in her chair. "I'm not imagining this. I had those dreams even before I met you. Believe me, because in my dreams you are dressed in a black velvet morning coat with a white ruffled shirt. I had quite a shock when I first saw you in the office. It's..." she hesitated and averted her gaze from mine, "it's enough to make me believe that we live more than once."

"That's fairytales. Wishful thinking."

"Then why the 19th century costumes and the opulent surroundings both of us dream about and cannot recognize?"

I shrugged. "Pure coincidence. Great imagination."

Gretchen studied me for a while in silence, then smiled and changed the subject.

I had orders to return to the States for a new assignment at Letterman Army Hospital at the Presidio of San Francisco and we left Germany three months after our wedding. We were given army housing, a duplex on a Presidio hill overlooking the Golden Gate Bridge. The island of Alcatraz in the middle of the Bay dominated the view and the circular dome of the Fine Arts Building, a remnant of the World's Fair Exposition in 1915, graced the landscape below us.

The hospital was a busy teaching center with a plethora of surgical patients and I plunged into my work with a single-minded dedication. I enjoyed being on the surgical teaching staff of the hospital, and had every reason to believe that if I worked hard, published medical articles and continued to get excellent efficiency reports from my superiors, my rank eventually would be raised to brigadier general. To that end I threw all my energies and thoughts.

*   *   *

It never occurred to me that Gretchen might not share my dual dedication to the army and to medicine. I had been used to my widowed mother's devotion to seeing me in medical school and sharing in my triumphs and failures. Although dying from leukemia my mother willed herself to linger long enough to see me near graduation. In my conviction that those who loved me would share in my drive toward my life's aim, I failed to notice Gretchen's angst because she tried hard to adapt to my tight schedule. She seemed willing enough to oblige when I asked her to give parties at home for residents and their wives—we had established close friendships then--and she enjoyed entertaining, preparing for them days in advance, always the perfectionist, the charming animated hostess. She loved clothes and I never scolded her for the large bills that came in every month from San Francisco stores, even though my army salary frequently was stretched to the breaking point. But I was proud of her and indulged her, ignoring petty annoyances at her extravagances. I understood her need of them, after living in near poverty after her father's death.

Our sex life was great, Gretchen's kittenish nature inflamed me. At times, she would take the initiative, trying for variety in lovemaking. I had to force myself not to succumb to vague suspicions, not to dwell on destructive thoughts. She had a captivating quality of being lavish with her praise. She often made endearing comments about my eyes, calling them blue jays, or ran her hand through my thick brown hair, or touched my forehead smoothing "surprise wrinkles" as she called them, in spite of the fact that she was 5'4" and I towered above her with my six foot frame.

At the end of my three-year assignment I was sent back to Germany, this time to Heidelberg. We enjoyed being in Europe again, and I was beginning to make a name for myself with the articles I wrote at night.

When Steve was born, we hired a German nanny, and life streamed forward content and serene. Or so I thought.

CHAPTER 3

During the early days of our marriage I still had those dreams about Gretchen in the mysterious period setting. Only now, she no longer danced in the ballroom but seemed preoccupied as she sat at an ornate Louis XV writing desk. Occasionally, she would lift her head and look at me with pained dark eyes. I did not like those dreams, which woke me up and made me reach for the red-headed flesh and blood Gretchen who slept beside me. I never told her about these later dreams and if she had them, she made no mention of hers.

About that time, an incident occurred which changed my outlook on life. I had to go to Nuremberg army hospital to deliver a lecture on surgical techniques I was developing and Gretchen went with me. We drove along the Neckar River, our road flanked on both sides by April apple and cherry blossoms and tender green pastures with grazing cattle on the banks. High on the rolling hills,Gray stone medieval castles, crumbling from neglect and damp from crawling moss, brooded above us. It was one of those perfect spring days when the bright blue sky and the burgeoning earth ready to bring forth reincarnated foliage filled my heart with buoyancy and vigor.

Happy and relaxed, I whistled as I drove the narrow German roads, occasionally glancing at Gretchen, radiant and beautiful beside me. Before long, she put her hand on my thigh and murmured, "Let's pull over into that orchard." She pointed in the direction of a grove of fruit trees, white blossoms hanging low over the earth, their scattered petals covering the ground.

My pulse quickened as I stopped on a dirt road and shut off the motor. We were surrounded by an archway of fragrant flowers as though we were in a natural gazebo somewhere in a large park. As I turned to sweep Gretchen into my arms, inhaling a mixture of her favorite *Blue Hour* perfume and the scent of the blossoms above, a tableau flashed in my mind's eye, equally beautiful, but from another era.

For a fleeting moment I saw myself leaning on the balustrade of a white-washed gazebo with stately ionic pillars, one hand nervously pulling at my thick sideburns. The dark-eyed Gretchen of my dreams in a black flowing gown stood facing me, tears streaming down her face, her arms in a suppliant gesture.

For some reason, this scene from the unknown past made me shudder, and I closed my eyes to shake it off. I ran my hands over Gretchen's silky head to reassure myself that I was still in the twentieth century. A sense of foreboding filled those dreams but I refused to dwell on them.

I gathered Gretchen into my arms and we made love. That interlude in an orchard could have been idyllic but soon the dark-haired woman of my dreams filled my inner vision again with such a provocative smile that I gave in to a frenzied lovemaking where Gretchen and the dark-haired beauty blended into one. Where only Gretchen's hands invaded and caressed before, her mouth dared to probe, explore, and capture.

The experience left me weak and bathed in perspiration from ecstasy, but also shock at the discovery that my seemingly uncomplicated wife was familiar with sexual techniques that I had only read about in textbooks.

Back on the twisting highway, I drove in silence for a long time, disturbed by conflicting emotions within me. She had given me the intense pleasure and yet...where had she acquired these sexual skills?

Finally, I cleared my throat. "Gretchen, where have you learned to make love like that?"

She threw me a sidelong glance. "Don't tell me you didn't enjoy it?"

I could feel my face redden. "That's beside the point. You haven't answered my question."

The corners of her mouth pulled down petulantly. "Your ego never ceases to amaze me, darling. You seem to have forgotten that I lived for twenty three years before I met you."

With a growing flush of anger, I gripped the wheel of the car and Gretchen, as if reading my thoughts, said, "Relax, silly. I was only teasing you."

There was a twinkle in her eye as she glanced at me again. "You have your textbooks and I have mine."

"What books?"

"Well, for starters, *The Ideal Marriage* by Van de Velde is a classic."

"Where in the world did you come across such a book?"

She shrugged. "I found it in my parents' bedroom a long time ago. I've been reading it ever since." She leaned her head on my shoulder and looked at me pointedly. "Can you blame me for wanting to try something different on you? After all, giving pleasure can be almost as exciting as receiving it."

My face grew warm and I concentrated on my driving. From that day on I saw Gretchen in a different light. At night, I sought new experiences in our intense lovemaking, while fighting the jealous twinge that nagged me with suspicion that Gretchen was not truthful with me.

*   *   *

After three years, the days of my assignment in Heidelberg was drawing to a close. Steve was a toddler, filling our house with chatter and activity. Our German nurse, Heidi, tall and busty, became like a member of our family, sharing our meals and going on our vacations with us, caring for and loving Steve like her own.

Gretchen spent many hours with her, talking to her inGerman, and although I warned her that she might pick up the crude dialect of a country girl, Gretchen only shrugged. "I'm better off talking to her than no one at all."

Ignoring the hint at my heavy work load, I let her go on, reluctant to disrupt the compatible atmosphere in the household. Although Gretchen did try to sympathize with the pressures of a surgeon's life and on many occasions asked how she could be of help, I consistently waved her away.

"Darling," she said once, "at least let me help you with sorting and filing your reports in your cabinet. That would give you some respite when you come home from a long day in surgery." She leaned over and kissed my forehead. "I'd fix you a martini and while you relax before dinner, I could put away your paperwork and file it the next day."

I couldn't imagine Gretchen handling my reports. I dismissed her with a weary 'no thanks' biting my tongue in time to keep myself from telling her that she had no medical training to understand how to file the complicated surgeries I performed. As time went on, we began to go our separate ways. Yet, she still tried to create a relaxing atmosphere at home by greeting me every evening with my favorite martini, but I took it as my due and the least she could do as a wife. My schedule left little time for leisure and Gretchen's pretense at being a good listener when I tried to share my successes with her, was painfully apparent. "You see," I said one afternoon after trying to tell her about an operation I performed on an old woman, "you aren't interested in my work at all. Look at you, starting to leaf through a *Theosophy* magazine while I am talking."

Gretchen raised her head and gave me an accusing stare. "And when was the last time you asked about *my* activities and show the slightest bit of interest in how I spend my days?"

"You know very well that I don't believe in Theosophy or reincarnation. I'm not a hypocrite to pretend I want to hear what you've learned on any given day."

"It doesn't take long to read this magazine. There's always time during the day to share our news and spend some time together. We live under the same roof, but we see each other only in passing. The only time we're together is at meals and at night, when we are--"

"That's enough!" I interrupted, afraid of what she might say about our sex life. I stalked out of the room and went outside to get some fresh air and calm myself. Our sex was still good, but had I become selfish in that as well? My face grew warm as I realized that Gretchen had become less passionate in response to my lovemaking, less enthusiastic about my approach.

I couldn't spend time wondering about that. My sick patient needed me and I had to return to the hospital. Married couples do have their spats occasionally, and I couldn't worry about that one. Nevertheless, a twinge of guilt wormed itself into my psyche but I shrugged it off and left the house.

*   *   *

We returned to San Francisco for another assignment at Letterman, but this time I didn't want to live on the Presidio grounds. Heidi had come with us and I wanted a larger home. We bought a house in a gated community in San Rafael, some twenty miles north of San Francisco and I commuted to the Presidio from there. It took me about twenty-five minutes to reach the hospital and I enjoyed those moments of peace behind the wheel of my car. I loved the area and loved owning our first home. When, after a couple of years at Letterman, I heard that an older surgeon decided to sell his practice in San Francisco, my yearning for promotion paled in the face of the temptation to settle down. I talked it over with Gretchen who was thrilled with the idea of living permanently near San Francisco, and I bought the surgeon's practice. Eventually I took in two partners and soon paid off our home. I did very well financially and indulged myself in my love of sports cars. I enjoyed my Porsche and Gretchen had a Mercedes.

During that time, she developed a deeper interest in the study of metaphysics and chattered about it every chance she got. Never a tidy person, she scattered her books all over our living room and family room tables. When I asked her where she got them, she told me that she frequented a metaphysical bookshop on Powell Street in San Francisco. I picked up a few from the coffee table and looked at the titles. There were books on yoga philosophy, on the power of thought, on theosophy, and an assortment of volumes on reincarnation and life after death.

What nonsense. "Do you seriously believe in all this stuff?" I asked.

She pursed her lips. "Don't put down something you know nothing about."

"Who started you on these books?"

She flipped her shoulder. "A friend."

"I can't believe you've fallen for this sort of thing."

She grabbed the books out of my hands and hugged them. "You've got your nose buried in your journals and that's all you care about." There were tears in her eyes. "You only deal with physical ailments. Someday you'll be sorry you didn't read my books."

I raised my hands. "God forbid."

"Listen to me!" Her voice rose. "There's a whole world out there that we don't see. Don't look so skeptical, damn it! I tell you, there *is* such a thing as fourth dimension with an energy field that we can tap into."

"And just how are we to achieve that?"

"By raising our consciousness to capture that energy."

I had a hard time keeping from laughing. "You can't be serious."

"Yes, I am. You don't know the least of it. For instance, we can't see our thoughts but they can affect our bodies. Even cure diseases. Take cancer, for instance, it--"

I could tell that she was on the verge of crying, and seeing her lovely face fighting for control, I felt a twinge of remorse. I realized that I wasn't giving her enough of my time, and if these books gave her some measure of satisfaction, who was I to ridicule it?

"O.K. Gretchen," I interrupted in a contrite voice, "I can see this means a lot to you." I put my arms around her and kissed her gently on the cheek. She leaned her head on my shoulder and sighed.

"Oh, Jim, if only you could spend more time with me. I know you are married to medicine, but could you think of me once in a while and take a day off when we could do something together?"

She raised her head and looked at me, her eyes glistening with gathering tears. I felt guilty and shamed. "I promise, darling, I'll try my best."

*　　*　　*

After that, Gretchen rarely mentioned her books or what she was learning from them. Once in a while, she'd get enthusiastic about the subject and talk about what she had discovered. All of it went over my head, but rather than argue, I would pretend to listen for a while, then smile, take her in my arms and kiss her on her mouth to stop the flow of esoteric words.

"Darling, you're becoming quite a philosopher," I said once while we were sitting in our family room sipping cocktails before dinner. "How about us taking in a movie after we eat? To lighten our minds a bit, eh?"

"You're not interested in what I'm studying," she retorted, wiggling out of my arms and giggling when I tickled her under the chin. "You think I'm not serious about it, but I *am*! Do you know that those who have had out of body experiences, say that they could simply wish themselves to any part of the world and be there in an instant?"

I laughed out loud. "Well then, just think, you and I could travel all over the world without standing in long lines at the airports!"

Gretchen slapped me on the hand and smiled in spite of herself. "Oh, you! You make fun of me."

"Not of you, but of the fairy tales you tell me. Come to think of it, I imagine it could be comforting to dream about such miracles."

Actually, I was glad that she had developed an interest of her own, irrational as it seemed to me. I felt free then to plunge deeper into my work, taking on more and more patients, performing a variety of more complex, more challenging surgical procedures, and building a fine reputation among my colleagues. Lulled into the complacency of daily routine,I assumed that Gretchen had finally become resigned to my heavy work load and went about her own interests and daily routine without complaining. She continued to be solicitous when I came home exhausted and tried to make me relax in the comfort of our home. We still had sex, but it had become sporadic and almost an obligatory function rather than romantic or passionate. I was unaware of the gathering darkness in my life.

*   *   *

How I wished now that I had listened to some of her comments about life after death. I cringed at the thought of having ridiculed

Gretchen's beliefs. I was reliving scenes from my past, haunting the physical world, then finding myself back in the out-of-body experience where I seemed to exist without knowing if it was to be permanent. I, Jim Braddock, a prominent surgeon, had become a drifter in time. I had lost everything I held dear in my life and was facing an uncertain future.

Images of the past faded, and all at once a flutter of anxiety quickened my breath. Steve. I remembered that he was driving an uninsured car to school. My God. I tried to tame my raging thoughts. Only yesterday he had come to me for advice and now I was powerless to give him whatever moral support he would need. It was its own kind of torture, this sense of impotency and frustration.

I forced myself to think of our conversation. After dinner I had gone to our family room and sat down in my comfortable rocker which had given me many pleasant hours in front of the fireplace. The brass filigree table lamp that at one time belonged to my mother was on, enveloping my rocker in a warm glow. I joined the tips of my fingers and rubbing my nose with the two index fingers, gazed at the dying embers in the fireplace. One of Gretchen's slippers was tucked under the sofa, the other lay upside down near the ottoman of her chair. A bowl with a few kernels of popcorn was left on the end-table. Steve must have wolfed it down earlier. Gretchen had never learned to like it.

Just as I started to read an article in the JAMA, Steve entered the room. He was wearing jeans and a plaid shirt with an open collar, his red hair thick and curly.

"What is it, son?" I said, laying down my medical journal and seeing his hesitation. "I'm listening."

Steve started to pace the floor. I leaned back in my chair, waiting.

"Out with it," I prodded gently.

"Dad, I never told you this, but there's a gang of four or five kids in our class who always get into trouble. They were suspended more than once already and I guess they're looking for an excuse to be thrown out of school."

"Who are they?"

Steve shrugged. "Oh, you wouldn't know them. They're just no good. They're into drugs all the way."

"What have they done?"

"In the past it was just little things, like getting into fights during recess, or carrying-on in class. One of them, Pete Foster, is a real bully. He seems to be the leader. He weighs a ton but it's all flab, so he never made the football team. Maybe he's getting even for that."

Steve stopped his pacing and faced me. "Dad, the other day after class, I stayed behind to do some lab work. I was standing at my locker across the hall when I saw all four of them run into the lab and the next thing I knew I heard a lot of noise in there. They were breaking glass tubes and laughing. I didn't stop them. I--I was scared."

Steve hesitated, and I waited.

"The principal made an announcement and said he's going to question everybody about it. I haven't told anyone, and I didn't want to. But, Dad, when the principal asks me directly, what do I say?"

"Steve you know the answer to that yourself. Dishonesty is never justified. Besides, what loyalty do you owe those boys? Are they your friends?"

Steve shook his head emphatically. "No. It's nothing like that. It's just that the guys saw me when I passed the lab on my way out. They'll know who squealed on them."

"If you lie to the principal, you'll become an accessory to the crime and your conscience will bother you, son."

"I can't rat on them."

"Are you scared of them?"

Steve couldn't meet my gaze and looked away. He picked up

Gretchen's slippers and placed them neatly by her chair. Then he straightened up and broke into a wide grin.

"I guess I knew all along what I have to do. I just wanted to hear it from you."

"We can't always avoid risks in life, son. Stay away from those boys as much as you can."

Steve nodded. Then with a resigned sigh, he turned to go out. At the door he paused, looked back at me as though he wanted to say something else, hesitated, shook his head and walked out.

That was only a few days ago but it seemed eons in the past. Tears stung my eyes. Like a small child yearning for a parent's comfort, I wanted to call up Dr. Farnsworth, but instead, I heard my colleagues' voices working over my inert body in the emergency room.

Where was Dr. Farnsworth? I wanted to talk to him.

"I'm right here, Jim," he said in answer to my unspoken question and I wheeled around to find myself back in the meadow, facing my teacher.

I rushed toward him. "I heard my colleagues' voices in the emergency room, but I'm still here. Why? I really don't want to die yet, I'm not ready. My son needs me. And I want to straighten things out between Gretchen and me."

Dr. Farnsworth raised his hand. "Whoa, Jim, slow down." He paused, and then said, "Look..."

As I looked in the direction he pointed, a wave of such supreme love washed over me that it caught my breath. A kind of love I had never experienced before, and it wasn't for Gretchen but for the golden vision of the woman I had seen earlier, whose vision now I couldn't see, but whose gentle voice strangely familiar, now spoke to me from a distance, "Paul, please listen to your heart..."

Again, as the last time, she faded into a mist, and Dr. Farnsworth was gone as well. I stood listening, wondering why she called me *Paul*.

I heard a sound, a rhythmic clip clop of horses' hoofs, at first barely discernible, then increasing in volume. I heard a man's voice urging the horses on and although he was using a language strange to my ears—throaty and sibilant—I understood what he was saying. I turned around.

CHAPTER 4

Through a thinning fog, I leaned forward to touch the coachman, and in doing so, received a blast of fresh air in my face. Although icy and as stinging as prickly needles, it was invigorating. In the next moment, I caught a whiff of horse, pungent and earthy and soon was able to distinguish the flowing muscles on the animal's glistening flanks. The horse exhaled a stream of white vapor with a loud snort, which melted the last of the fog. I squinted from the glare of the snow that was all around me.

I was seated in a small open sleigh, one of three such sleighs following a larger, covered one ahead. I knew instantly who and where I was. My name was Count Paul Uvarov, an aide to Tsar Alexander II of Russia, whom I greatly admired. I was even aware of the date: Sunday, March 13, 1881. We were in St. Petersburg, returning to the Winter Palace from the nearby Manège where the Tsar attended the trooping of the colors. Although this was a routine Sunday event, this particular Sunday it held a special significance for the Tsar: his young nephew, Dmitri, the son of his favorite brother, Constantine, had taken part in the parade for the first time as an aide-de-camp to His Majesty.

Earlier that morning at the Winter Palace, an event took place that I hoped would make this Sunday an historic one. I had no way of knowing that in a few minutes a far different event would imprint this Sunday in history books. But at the moment, I was thinking of the scene I had witnessed in the Tsar's study that morning. Premier, General Loris-Melikov, had brought in a manifesto prepared for the Tsar's signature. It decreed the summoning of representatives of various social classes to render service to the state council. It was the first step toward a progressive government and, I hoped, would eventually lead toward a constitutional monarchy.

The Tsar's father, Nicholas I, was a stern despot who ruled the country with an iron fist. He inherited the throne after the death of his elder brother, Tsar Alexander I, called the Blessed for conquering Napoleon in 1812. Young aristocrats who followed the Tsar on his triumphant entry to Paris were fired up by the revolutionary spirit in France and returned to Russia full of dangerous ideas. They wanted to overthrow the Tsar's autocratic rule and create a constitutional monarchy. They chose to revolt on December 14, 1825, shortly after Alexander I died and before Nicholas I was crowned. Their attack was poorly planned and in the skirmish that followed, they were caught and imprisoned. The new Tsar dealt harshly with the rebels. Five conspirators were executed and the rest were exiled to Siberia for life. Later, they were called The Decembrists.

The Tsar's son and heir, the present Alexander II, witnessed the revolt, his father's harsh treatment of the guilty aristocrats, and his subsequent tight control of the country. Honorable, gentle by nature, Alexander II could see that his father's rule was akin to a police state. After Nicholas' death, Alexander pardoned the Decembrists, but they were not allowed to live in Moscow or St. Petersburg and were under surveillance for the rest of their lives.

The Tsar, hailed as the Tsar-Liberator, had abolished serfdom in 1861, but it had only stirred up unrest in the country. Having lost the security and protection of the landowners, the peasants, still woefully poor and ignorant of the responsibilities attached to their freedom, rioted and demanded further concessions. I could hardly blame them. They were each given a small piece of land to work with, but not for free —they had to pay for it over a two-year period. I was a landowner myself and secretly criticized the Tsar for passing a law, altruistic and humane as it was (no more splitting up the serfs' families and selling individuals like cattle to other landowners), without insisting on accompanying reforms in the lower echelons of bourgeoisie.

Several attempts on the Tsar's life, mostly by radical students, had resulted in his having to be heavily guarded. Today, he was accompanied by six Terek Cossacks, one sitting next to the coachman, the others riding alongside. The Tsar's covered sleigh was followed by three others, the district police master Colonel Adrian Dvorzhitsky's, two officers' of the gendarmerie, and finally my own. The Tsar resented this protection and only gave in to it because of his family's repeated pleadings. Once I overheard him say, "If I am not safe on the streets with this much protection, then I might as well abdicate."

The Tsar's marriage was an arranged one and for years remained courteous and amicable. After the Empress died, he entered into a morganatic marriage with his longtime mistress, Princess Ekaterina Dolgorukaya, giving her a new name of Princess Yurievskaya. The Tsar glowed with happiness and I was glad for him. The marriage, however, didn't add to his popularity either. In making public his love affair with a woman young enough to be his daughter, the Tsar alienated his immediate family as well.

Love affairs at Court were almost de rigueur among the aristocracy, and I was a party to them myself. We had an unwritten law however, that outward pretenses of fidelity had to be maintained. It was a game we all played to perfection. My own involvement with the dark-eyed Baroness Irene Goulevskaya was a classic example. At thirty I was still a bachelor, and pleased to remain one, but the gentleman's code of honor dictated proper behavior in public toward the Baroness. Her aging husband, a highly decorated military campaigner, had retired to his estates and was content to allow his young wife to remain at Court as a lady-in-waiting to one of the Grand Duchesses.

I was careful to pursue only married women, both for the spice of conquest and the safety from deeper entanglement. My dark eyes were always on the lookout for a pretty woman. I knew that my slim figure and blond hair were enhanced by my Izmailovsky Regiment dress uniform with white breeches and green tunic laced with gold, and I took full advantage of it.

Falling in love was as easy for me as changing uniforms and I had no desire for lasting relationships. I already had a deep attachment that offered me loyalty and devotion. My beautiful young sister, Nadine, dark-haired and blue-eyed, was twenty-eight and the light of my life. I tolerated her husband, Arkady, an officer in the Preobrazhensky Guards. Because of his noble birth and great wealth, he offered Nadine protection and security that I couldn't provide as a bachelor brother. But our souls belonged to each other, of that I was sure, and no intruder could sever that bond. I had dabbled in mysticism in earlier days—it was fashionable then—vaguely believing in reincarnation and fancying myself some medieval lord who had loved Nadine over many centuries. With only two years' difference in our ages, we were playmates since early childhood. As an older brother, I engaged her in childish pranks and gladly took the punishment for our mischief. We romped around the huge park on our estate, playing hide and seek near the marble gazebo, or, as we grew older, galloped on our stallions racing along the tree-lined lanes.

We were educated at home by private tutors as was the custom among the nobility, and Nadine often came to my study asking for help with her school work. When it was time for me to join the Izmailovsky Guards and serve the Tsar, I visited our Otradnoye estate as often as

I could. After Nadine turned eighteen and was presented at Court, Arkady, then just retired with honors from the military and one of the counselors to the Tsar, asked our parents for Nadine's hand.

Already in his forties with a weather-beaten face and graying hair, a widower with no children, he presented a less than dashing figure, but our parents felt that it would be an enviable match and gave their consent. To my surprise, Nadine did not object and seemed content if not obviously happy to marry the man. I questioned her docile acceptance and she said, "My dear, my own Paul, I have accepted an honorable and well-placed man who seems to adore me. I prefer to have the security of his love rather than become an old maid or seek out a younger, handsome man who could soon tire of me and cause me pain." Then she said a strange thing that I understood only much later, "I could never fall in love with anyone – of that I am sure. Besides, I am quite fond of Arkady." She looked at me with tears in her eyes and ran out of the room. I stood there, confused by her words and dreading the day when she would be gone from our beloved Otradnoye.

During her engagement, our parents were killed when their carriage hit a boulder and overturned. Mother died at the scene and Father a few days later. It was now up to me to be the one to give Nadine away at her wedding. Whenever I think about it, a pain stabs my stomach like a burning ulcer. Tall and regal in her bearing, wearing a white silk dress trimmed with lace, a diadem on her head over the veil, she was more beautiful than I had ever seen her.

When the wedding was over and it was time for the bride and groom to kiss, Arkady took Nadine into his arms and kissed her on the mouth. As I watched her put her arms around his neck and return his kiss, my body went on fire with such a yearning ache, that I caught my breath. I staggered out into the fresh air and stood shocked at my reaction. The true nature of my love for Nadine existed under the thin layer of brotherly affection, never to be exposed or acknowledged by me. But my disloyal body had betrayed me then, and I understood what Nadine had meant when she said that she could never fall in love with anyone. This kind of love between us was mutual – unspoken, incestuous, and forbidden.

Nadine remained my friend and confidante, whom I trusted implicitly. We never spoke of the love that smoldered between us.

Not so with Irene. I was beginning to tire of the baroness and the more demanding she became of my time, the cooler I grew toward her. Her recent behavior at the ball of the Palm Trees at the Palace was a case in point.

The evening had started auspiciously. One hundred carefully nurtured palm trees had been brought by horse-drawn carts from the Tsarskoe Selo Palace and specially constructed round tables, each seating fifteen people, were placed around the bases of these trees.

The Tsar and his wife, Princess Yurievskaya, opened the ball to the rhythm of the Blue Danube waltz. They made an elegant pair, he – tall with dazzling blue eyes, and she – dark-haired and fragile looking. After fourteen years of liaison and one of marriage, they still looked like newlyweds. Both were dressed in white, she in a moiré gown with blue velvet accents and he in a long white tunic trimmed with blue fox.

"Lovely, aren't they?"

Startled, I looked down into the blue eyes of my beloved sister, Nadine. What a mockery of fate that she was my sibling! And because of that I had to suppress my yearning for her by pursuing other women.

How different she was from Princess Yurievskaya! Taller than most women, statuesque and voluptuous, Nadine glowed with vitality. Dressed in blue velvet to offset her dark hair, she knew well how to show off her beauty to the best advantage. Her skin was translucent and because of that her blue eyes always seemed to sparkle with warmth. I often wondered how men could resist the mocking scrutiny of her eyes. That night they shone with a special intensity I had not seen before, and her usually pale cheeks were glowing with color.

"They certainly are," I said glancing at the royal couple and pressing gently into her waistline, "but not as lovely as my sister I hold captive right now."

Nadine threw her head back and laughed lightly. "You are prejudiced, Paul." She fanned herself with a mother-of-pearl fan. "It's very warm in here. Let's move into the parlor. It should be cooler there and besides, I want to talk to you."

"Oh, oh, sounds like another lecture coming up. What have I done?"

"What am I going to do with you? Are you ever going to be serious?"

"Serious about what?"

"About life, silly. You exasperate me. I don't know how your future wife is going to put up with you."

As we went through the door into the parlor, I leaned over Nadine's ear and whispered, "I've got a little secret for you, *ma soeur*, I don't ever intend to get married."

"Why not?"

I made a mock bow. "Since I'll never find a woman as thoroughly enticing as you, little one, I shall remain a bachelor forever." I often engaged in this banter to cover up my true feelings and that evening was no exception.

A sad smile touched Nadine's lips. "You shouldn't speak such nonsense. The Court is filled with lovely women. Nothing would make me happier than to see you safely married."

"Safely? Am I in danger? Married to whom?"

"Well, certainly not to Irene. She's already married. And while on the subject of Irene–"

"We're *not* on the subject of the baroness. Why bring her up?" My voice sounded sharper than I had intended it to be, so I patted Nadine's hand and smiled, but she withdrew her arm.

"Because you're acting shamefully toward her. It's bad enough that you are involved with a married woman, but now that you managed to achieve your conquest and she has fallen in love with you, you're treating her disgracefully."

I shrugged. "She's a married woman and knows what she's doing. I never intended it to become a *grand passion*. Besides, I don't like clinging vines, you know that."

"Paul, how can you be so callous?"

"I'm only pragmatic."

"No. You're cold and disinterested, and that's even worse."

"What would you have me do? Challenge her old husband to a duel when I don't even love her?"

The thought of my fighting a duel with a tottering old man was so ludicrous that I laughed. Nadine's eyes blazed.

"How can you take someone else's suffering so lightly, especially since you're the cause of it?"

My guard slipped and I took Nadine by her elbows. "God, but you're beautiful tonight."

Nadine threw my hands off and stepped back. "Stop changing the subject when you don't want to be scolded. I'm well aware of this trick of yours. I'm your *sister*, remember?"

"Yes, I do remember. I only wish I could forget." My voice thickened. "There's my punishment."

Slowly, Nadine's face reddened and she averted her eyes. "We're treading on dangerous ground, Paul. Let's change the subject."

"Then what is it that you want me to do?"

"I want you to stop playing cat-and-mouse game with Irene. Tell her gently that you don't love her." Nadine clenched her fists. "Stop seeing her alone. It's not fair to her."

Nadine's last words were choked with emotion. I thought I saw her lips quiver. She turned away and pressed a handkerchief against her mouth.

"Nadine, dearest, let's not argue over silly things. I can well handle the situation. You shouldn't concern yourself with it. Let's go back in."

Nadine resisted. "Promise me that you'll end your affair with Irene before it goes too far."

"You always end up having it your way, don't you? Very well, then, I promise."

Nadine smiled a tired smile. "Thank you. You've always kept your promises to me. Thank you, dear one."

She patted my cheek with her gloved hand, refused my proffered arm and walked back into the ballroom, leaving me standing alone at the entrance to the ballroom. I heard a movement to my left and saw Irene standing in the shadow behind a column. Her hand trembled as she fanned herself and her dark eyes were awash with tears. She looked at Nadine with unconcealed hatred and instinctively I blocked the door, but she shook her head and walked away.

Later, after Nadine had gone home and I was leaving the ball, Irene confronted me in one of the empty salons. I bowed low over her hand and paid her a banal compliment. She flushed. "Thank you, Count Uvarov, but I no longer need it." Her formal tone surprised me.

"You're welcome." Instantly, I felt foolish for my inappropriate response but she dismissed it with a wave of her hand.

"I doubt that I shall ever speak to you again except in public." Irene's eyes were at once accusing and sad. "From now on our contacts will only be those required by Court Protocol."

I could hardly believe my ears. Irene was actually saving me the unpleasantness of breaking up our affair. I should have accepted her words graciously but instead, my curiosity was aroused and my ego smarted. I raised my brows and said, "Just what have I done to deserve such a drastic change of heart?"

Irene did not waver. "Call it suspicion, intuition, whatever, but it's all over between us."

"I don't understand what you are hinting at."

"I'm sure you do. The only thing that you don't realize is that your behavior is rather transparent."

"You're speaking in riddles, Irene, making accusations without having the courage to spell them out."

"Very well, then. Your personal life is causing gossip at Court and it has nothing to do with me."

Vaguely uncomfortable, I forced a chuckle. "Please continue, you're still being unclear."

"Tonight you didn't speak to me at all. You behaved as though I wasn't there." Irene's voice faltered. "I watched how you talked and danced with your sister. How you looked at her. This was not the first time I've seen this. And I overheard part of your conversation with her tonight. Need I say any more?"

Now I knew. There was no doubt to what she was referring.

"I can't believe what I'm hearing." I was choking with anger. "Your jealousy knows no bounds. How dare you throw suspicion on an innocent person?"

"There's no need to raise your voice."

I hadn't realized that I was losing my temper. I clenched my fists in an effort to steady my voice. Irene was pale but remained calm.

"I referred to no one but you. My own feelings on the matter are private, but I'm well aware of how illicit are yours."

"You're the last person to play the role of righteous indignation.

What right do you have to accuse someone who has never been touched by scandal?"

"It remains to be seen. I'm giving you a fair warning, Paul. One of these days your actions will boomerang and hurt the very people you love the most."

"And what qualifies you, Baroness, to preach to me? Are you so saintly yourself?"

"I don't claim to be perfect, but at least I don't cross the boundaries of natural law."

There was unabashed contempt in Irene's last words, and it hit its mark. I hated her. With a singular intensity, I hated her.

*   *   *

I was so deep in my thoughts reliving my recent confrontation with the baroness, that I hadn't noticed when we turned into *St. CatherineStreet* along the *Catherine Canal Quay*. Momentarily surprised that we didn't follow the usual route along the *Malaya Sadovaya Street*, I remembered that the Tsar had called on his cousin, the Grand Duchess Catherine, daughter of his uncle Michael, and today the cortège was taking an alternate route back to the Palace.

I surveyed the scene with boredom; I had seen it so many times before.

The snow on the ground was packed from winter's many months of frost, browned by pedestrians' feet and the sleighs' rungs. Stone wall and iron spikes along the canal looked forbidding and cold. A few straggly trees, shorn through the autumn of their golden foliage, stood immobilized in their nakedness, barely supporting a few puffs of old snow. The fresh blanket of winter that had covered the street's drabness and gave it an ephemeral aura of purity in early November, had long since dissolved into the seediness and melancholy of the northern frost. The St. Petersburg spring had not yet rejuvenated nature.

Gawking passers-by, some with silly grins at the unexpected pleasure of seeing the royal carriage, gaped at us, while others hurried along the quay, speeding up their steps at the sight of the police and mounted Cossacks. A boy ran across the street in front of the Tsar's carriage. A young man holding a parcel in his hands was leaning idly against the railing of the canal, and I wondered what he was doing there on such a cold day.

As we proceeded along the canal, the Cossacks trotting on both sides of the imperial coach, a thick-set youth in a fur hat ran forward and threw a package between the legs of the Tsar's horses. A loud explosion drew me to my feet, and I leaned to one side to see around Colonel Dvorzhitsky's sleigh to the Tsar's coach. Shards of glass glistened on the snow and a bluish smoke rose from the spot. Two horses lay torn apart, and the splintered door of the Tsar's coach was dangling on its hinges. A Cossack lay dead on the ground.

Oh, my God, the Tsar! But as the terrifying thought pierced my mind, the Tsar alighted from the carriage. He seemed slightly dazed but otherwise unhurt. The police had already grabbed the would-be assassin. The Tsar, in his sapper's uniform and plumed hat walked over to him.

"Who are you, young man?" he asked.

"A student."

"What's your name?"

"Nikolai Rysakov," the young man replied sullenly omitting the required 'Your Majesty'.

The Tsar seemed not to notice the young man's defiance.

"How old are you?"

"Nineteen."

The Tsar shook his finger at Rysakov and turning to look around him, walked over to an adolescent boy who moments ago had been watching his sovereign coach ride by and now was gurgling blood in his death throes. Colonel Dvorzhitsky approached the Tsar.

"Are you all right, Your Majesty?"

The Tsar nodded and pointed to the dying boy. "I'm not hurt, thank God, but he…"

Rysakov, firmly held by the gendarmerie, spoke in a barely audible voice but since he was standing near my sled, I overheard him.

"It's a little early to thank God."

I turned in his direction and saw the youth who had been leaning on the railing, suddenly come alive. With one arm high above his head, he stepped forward and threw the parcel he was holding at the Tsar's feet.

This time the explosion threw me out of the sleigh, and as I fell, I was hit by a large flying object. After I picked myself up, grateful for being unhurt, I looked down and recoiled. It was a human leg.

Several people lay on the ground moaning. Huge puddles of blood were spreading over the snow, soaking into it like red ink into a blotter.

The Tsar half-lay, half-sat against the canal railing. He was bareheaded. Thin rivulets of blood were running down his face which was peppered with tiny wounds. His uniform was in shreds, his abdomen torn open with a yawning wound. The left leg was broken and lay at an angle, and the right one—I began to shake—the right one was mangled to a pulp. Blood pulsed from his groin, soaking his uniform and the snow around him.

Colonel Dvorzhitsky and I reached the Tsar at the same time. The Tsar pointed toward me with his hand.

I stared at it – one finger was missing.

Then I heard his whisper, hoarse and barely audible.

"Home to the palace…to die…there…it's so cold…"

As I lifted his shoulders, he lost consciousness. Shaking with sobs, I helped move the Tsar into Colonel Dvorzhitsky's sleigh, and when we did so, I saw that the colonel was wounded too. I turned to look for the second assassin and saw with macabre satisfaction that he had been blown to pieces.

At the Winter Palace, officers and servants helped us carry the Tsar up the marble stairs into his study, huge drops of blood leaving a trail behind us. We lowered him gently on the couch by his desk. I heard weeping and prayers outside the door, but knew that there was no hope. The Tsar was dying.

Three doctors busied themselves over him and I retreated toward the corner of the room, wanting to help but not knowing what to do.

The room began to fill with the Imperial family. No one spoke. The 36-year old heir to the throne, the Grand Duke Alexander, stood by the window. A huge man, tall and muscular, his strength was phenomenal. It was rumored that when provoked, he could bend and twist a silver spoon. The thick fingers of his right hand were playing absent-mindedly with the braid of his uniform as he stared at the scene below the windows. I followed his gaze.

Thousands of people were near the palace, many knelt on the ground, heads bowed in silent prayer. The Preobrazhensky guards stood with bayonets fixed in belated vigil. The crowds were orderly and silent, sensing instinctively, that the dreaded announcement would soon be made.

Inside the room, the quiet was shattered by a door thrown open. Princess Yurievskaya burst into the study, and screaming "Sasha, Sasha," threw herself over his inert body, kissing his hands and sobbing hysterically. The doctors tried to pull her off, but she clawed at them and fought them with fists. In the end, they left her alone. A few minutes later the Tsar died, and she slid down to the floor in a faint, her pink negligée crimson with blood.

Grand Duchess Maria Fedorovna who, until then stood motionless as if fused to the floor in a far corner of the room, walked over to her husband, Alexander, who was now the new Tsar. She always wore her dark hair pulled tightly back on the sides with curls piled high on the top to accentuate her delicate features. The Grand Duchess was a vivacious and fun-loving woman, and it was difficult to believe the rumor that her sister, Princess Alexandra, the wife of the Prince of Wales, was more beautiful than she. At the moment however, the Grand Duchess Maria Fedorovna was ashen and her trembling caused the gentle tinkling of a pair of skates which she still held in her hand.

Everyone was in a state of shock, and I felt an intruder in the family grief. Tiptoeing out of the study, I walked aimlessly through the grand rooms of the palace.

I was dazed myself, unable to accept the tragedy that the first truly liberal Tsar, the hope of Russia, was gone. Ever since the Tsar liberated the serfs in 1961 and introduced new reforms in the country, a group of young revolutionaries who wanted to do away with the autocratic rule of the Tsars saw Alexander II as a threat to their cause. The Tsar escaped several attempts on his life until this tragic day. I was well aware that the new Tsar Alexander III, although present at the signing of the Manifesto that morning, strongly disapproved of his father's liberal reforms. The fate of the Manifesto was now at stake. Would he, as the new Tsar, in spite of his personal opposition, respect his father's wishes and proceed with its publication or would his near-sighted vision of his country's needs overrule his filial devotion and cause him to suppress it?

I paused in the grand ballroom, which only a few nights earlier had been the scene of exquisite luxury and festivity. The glamorous

Tsar, then so happy and gracious, walked among his guests, drinking champagne and charming his subjects with his kindly and witty remarks.

I sat down in that same ballroom now empty of human sounds, until the afternoon light faded. For a while, grief and apprehension paralyzed me, then suddenly I felt I had to get out of there. As I turned to leave, I came face to face with Irene. There was such horror in her eyes that in spite of myself, I felt sorry for her. I knew that she was a close friend of Princess Yurievskaya, and must have just come from her apartments.

"What a heartbreak for all of us, a tragedy for Russia, *ma chère*," I said kissing her ice-cold hand. But her eyes stared beyond my face at some phantom visible only to her. She shook her head slowly. "Oh, Paul, how dreadful, how shameful the whole thing is. The cruelty... the callousness...I can't understand it..."

Irene trembled and her breath came in short little gasps. I patted her hand.

"I know, *ma chère*, I know. I was there with the Tsar when it happened."

"Not the Tsar!" Irene's voice rose hysterically. "His Highness, the Grand Duke. How could he be so cruel, so totally without feeling?"

Irene buried her face in her hands. "I can't bear to think of it."

I frowned. "What are you talking about? Which Grand Duke? What happened?"

Irene's eyes brimmed with tears. "Our new Tsar's brother, Vladimir. His father's body isn't cold yet and he's already taking over."

"Pull yourself together, Irene. Tell me what happened."

She swallowed hard, wiped her eyes and clutched her hands together in an effort to keep them from shaking. I waited. When she spoke, her voice was breaking.

"I was waiting for Princess Yurievskaya when she was carried into her boudoir. Her negligée was smeared with the Tsar's blood." Irene closed her eyes and shuddered. "I helped undress her and put her to bed, but as soon as she regained consciousness, she became very agitated. She begged me to go to the Tsar's desk and find the Manifesto that he had signed this morning. She was afraid that the new Tsar would want it destroyed."

"What right does the Princess have to interfere in the affairs of State?"

"Don't you see? It was important to her to save the one thing that the Tsar believed in and wanted to do."Irene paused and began to pace the floor. "I was too late. I saw Grand Duke Vladimir walk out of the room with the manifesto in his hand. He wouldn't do it on his own. The new Tsar......"Irene began to cry. "The Princess...she–she became hysterical when I told her."

I stared at her in dismay. I never dreamed that Alexander would defy his father's wishes so quickly. Surely, out of respect for the Tsar's memory... Slow realization took hold of me. A despotic autocrat would sit on the throne of Russia again and play right into the hands of the revolutionaries. Far from liberating the country from autocratic rule, the assassin had set the country back into the Dark Ages.

My anger against Irene melted away in the face of our common tragedy and I put my arm around her shoulders in our silent grief and fear for the future of our country.

I don't know how long we stood like that, locked in a quiet embrace before Irene stopped shaking and moved away from me.

"Thank you," she said quietly. "I am so frightened for Russia. What is to become of all of us? Oh, Paul," she clutched my arms, "Whatever our differences, we both love our *rodina–our motherland*. Stay with the new Tsar, influence him. You believe in the constitutional monarchy. The more people like you surround the new Tsar, the better our chances of success."

I disliked Alexander intensely. He was a stubborn autocrat who treated his father's reforms with silent disapproval. What possible influence could I exert on him? I was not a diplomat, not his counselor. I didn't want to be near him and watch him destroy all the reforms that his father had introduced over the years of his reign. The iron fist of Tsar Nicholas I was re-emerging in the grandson.

Irene was shaking me. "Please, Paul... You must! You must!"

The pulse pounded in my temples threatening to explode in my brain. *The Tsar I loved is dead. His kindness and concern for the innocent dying boy and even the assassin, had cost him his life. If only he had remained in his coach and hurried away, he would be alive now. If only... Ah! What's the use!*

My eyes clouded and the whole room with Irene in it, began to tumble before me like scrambled pieces of a kaleidoscope. Nausea rose to my throat. I lost my footing and began to fall forward into another time.

CHAPTER 5

Thrown into vertigo of forward thrust, I had nothing to hold onto. A crawling sensation on my neck and face made me shudder as if an army of insects and slithering creatures were invading me. Terrified, I wiped my face and neck with my hands, but felt nothing. I found myself in a void, but as my eyes became accustomed to darkness, I could see that the total blackness surrounding me was in perpetual motion – great sweeping waves that rolled and pounded around me like a stormy sea at night. Gradually, I was caught up in a whirlpool of black smoke so dense I wondered why I wasn't choking.

A cacophony of sounds started up and sent a ripple of gooseflesh down my back. A screeching of animals in pain mixed with plaintive human moans of great suffering echoed through the darkness. Close to my ears they gathered, receding dolefully into the distance and winging back like a pendulum, one overlapping the other until I pressed my hands to my ears and let out a cry that reverberated in my brain like an explosive thunder.

I tumbled over and over without gravity into space and into silence. It was a disturbing silence, filled with threat and foreboding. Then the darkness around me took on a transparent quality. Nothing moved. The quiet and the stillness of this void taunted, threatened and drove me to a pitch of anxiety so great that I thrashed with my legs trying to get a foothold on the ground. Instead, I was weighted down by heaviness, as if the ills of the whole world had descended upon me. I felt ailing and aged and as I looked down on my hands, they became gnarled and shriveled with bulging veins moving about like busy worms.

Was this hell?

Unable to escape, I sobbed, waved my arms in the black void, pushed at emptiness.

Suddenly my mother's words rang in my ears, 'Think strongly of a place you want to be and you'll be there instantly.'

Afraid to move, I shut my eyes tightly, desperate to get away from this place for there was no longer any doubt in my mind that I had been pulled into the macabre sphere of the lower astral plane.

Even before I summoned courage to look, I felt a perceptible change in the atmosphere and knew that my effort worked. A wave of warmth and peace welled within me, lifting the oppressive weight and gifting me with renewed energy.

Fear vanished and into that silence came a sound. At first so faint that I dared not hope it was real, it grew in volume and presently I recognized the sonorous chords of an organ. Plangent and rhythmic, they penetrated the veil that engulfed me, and blinking, I opened my eyes and looked at my hands. They were normal again, the hands I knew so well, the hands that belonged to James Braddock, M.D., respected, self-assured surgeon. Self-assured? More like arrogant, I realized now. I laughed out loud, and heard an echo tinged with hysteria. Not only arrogant, but selfish, turning a blind eye to the needs of my family. This dreadful experience I had just had was a sure reminder of what I had become. Ashamed of allowing my emotions to get the better of me, I closed my mouth to choke down the forced laughter.

How was that Russian life connected to my present one? Too

much was thrown at me at once and I wanted to get back to my physical life, to rekindle the closeness with Gretchen, spend more time with her and Steve. Instead, I stared into nothing.

Little by little, I became aware that I was standing in a richly furnished room of the Louis XIV period. Men dressed in velvet and silk coats with lace cuffs, women in long padded skirts heavily embroidered in gold, buckled shoes and powdered wigs moved about the room murmuring softly, the swishing of the skirts gentle on the ear. The air was warm and permeated with a mixture of strong perfumes, the scent of roses and lavender predominant in the room.

Was I hallucinating? I shook my head to clear my vision, but the image remained. I wondered if a masquerade party was in progress with people dressed in elaborate costumes. Yet they seemed to fit in with the decor of the room. I didn't belong here in my utilitarian business suit of the modern world.

I studied the furnishings carefully and it became apparent that I was in a magnificent palace. Along the silk paneled walls Louis XIV chairs lined the parlor like a row of gilded palace guards. Near them stood a commode of inlaid wood, intricately designed in checkerboard pattern and heavily encrusted with ormolu.

The colors were intense and as I peered closer, I discovered that the commode consisted of a myriad of tiny particles that swirled and vibrated so rapidly that from a distance they appeared motionless and fused into a firm piece of wood. The effect was spectacular and without thinking, I reached down and ran my hand over the sparkling surface of the black marble top. It felt smooth and cool.

Surprised, I turned to look for the Professor. He was sitting in a red velvet chair with his legs crossed and his arms folded. It was comforting to see him wearing a herringbone gray jacket, white shirt with a red tie and navy slacks.

"Welcome back, Jim," he said before I could ask about the commode.

I walked over and lowered myself heavily in the chair next to him. "I know what hell is like, Professor. I've just been there."

"I know," he said. "The power of thought is awesome, Jim. You've been surrounded by the sum total of your negative thoughts and emotions. And that's the real hell. Do you want to talk about it?"

"No!" I had never thought of myself as a coward, but now I dreaded even thinking about that place for fear I might be pulled back into it. In this dimension, I had no guarantee that it wouldn't happen again, so I changed the subject.

"What was the significance of the Russian scenes I've just relived, Professor?"

"You'll find out in due time, Jim."

I couldn't sit still. I rose and inadvertently pushed a small end table that stood near the chair. As it tilted, I grasped its round top by the gold frame in which it was encased. Its smooth inlaid wood surface sparkled at me like the black marble top of the commode. I wheeled to face the professor. "It's alive!"

The professor laughed. "Not really. But quite spectacular, don't you think?"

He was right. As I had already discovered, everything there was in perpetual motion. Even inanimate objects. It would be impossible to describe all this to someone in the physical world.

I looked at the end table again. I didn't like its gold frame. Too ornate for my taste. How would it be without it, I wondered. I visualized the dainty, curved legs and the inlaid wood top framed in its own wood with a darker shade rounding the corners. As I concentrated on the image, suddenly the table blurred in front of my eyes and the one I created in my mind appeared in its stead. I gasped.

Bending over it quickly, I ran my trembling hand over it to make sure it was real and solid. It was.

Shaken, I stepped back. I had already learned that by a strong wish I could instantly be in another place, but creating objects by the same means... Was it just a fluke? Could I do it again? I closed my eyes and visualized a roll top desk I had always wanted for my den but never got around to buying. It had to be of heavy oak with many slots for letters and notes, and a secret drawer hidden somewhere inside. I smiled at my fancy and opened my eyes. My heart pounded both from delight and a weird feeling of being in some sort of surreal world. Surely I was participating in a clearly defined dream, for there before me, stood a roll top desk exactly as I had imagined it.

"Professor, is this for real?" I said turning to him.

"It's very real," he replied. "You'll learn a lot of things while you are in this dimension."

I looked at the desk again. Without realizing it, I had just created a desk by the power of my thought. *Power of my thought?* I shuddered. This meant that thoughts lived somewhere, biding their time, waiting to be reinforced by good or evil intentions. I just had such an experience in the quagmire of my negative thoughts. When my patients failed to respond to treatment, I sometimes told them to think positive thoughts, and quoted Norman Cousins who said that laughter helped the healing process. Yes, to my patients I preached, forgetting to do some housecleaning in the dark chambers of my own mind.

The sudden revelation began to chip at the veneer of my self-confidence, leaving me exposed to seeing what I really was – intolerant of others' weaknesses. In essence – a prig and a pompous ass. I winced and suddenly laughed out loud at my own assessment. At least I was being honest with myself. Still, I wanted to hide from professor's understanding smile. Oh, how I hoped and prayed, yes, prayed now that my colleagues would succeed in reviving me. I could heal and emerge a different man.

Someone was still playing the organ in the next room, this time a gentle, soothing melody. Questions hop-scotched in my brain. "Professor, who are these masquerading people?"

"They're not masquerading, Jim. They don't belong to the twentieth century. It's just as natural for them to wear red knee-high socks, black shoes with red high heels, wigs, and lace-trimmed shirts, as it is for us to be in our business suits."

"But we *are* in the twentieth century, Professor," I insisted. "It seems ridiculous to stagnate in a period that belongs to history."

"Nothing stagnates here, Jim. As for the twentieth century, time here is not measured in terms of centuries. The early seventeen hundreds are just as real to these people as when they lived in the physical world."

Professor Farnsworth looked at me whimsically. "What would you say if I told you that two lifetimes back you walked among them and thought yourself quite elegant when you sported a red-plumed hat at the Court of Louis XIV of France?"

I gaped at the professor. The image of me dressed in brocaded coat with lace-frilled shirt and wig with cascading curls was so incongruous that I burst out laughing. "You're kidding me."

He smiled. "Not at all. You were a respected physician in that life as well, although not a surgeon. In those days, surgery was considered to be only a craft and you looked down upon surgeons with disdain."

I cleared my throat. "So, that's why this time I chose surgical specialty!"

More and more Gretchen's words kept surfacing in my mind. "Cause and effect," she had said to me once, "what you sow, so shall you reap."

The professor smiled. "During the reign of the Sun King," he said,

"Guy-Crescent Fagon was appointed the king's physician in 1693. You were one of his assistants and remained at Court until the king's death in 1715. Come, meet the good doctor."

He led me toward a caricature of a man standing primly on his spindly legs against the wall. His powdered face with rouged cheeks was framed by thick and black curls of his wig that reflected a raven glint from the flickering candles in the sconces above his head. Nestled under a long humped nose, his thick red lips were compressed into an expression of bad after-taste, while his hooded eyes studied me with frank amusement. A strong smell of lavender mixed with something less pleasant wafted from him. Of course, I thought, these people lived in the seventeenth century and plumbing and showers were far in the future. Perfume dealers ran a prosperous business in those days, for sure. I suppressed a chuckle.

As I watched him, facts and names began to tumble into my brain. Fagon. The self-appointed authority on all medical matters and chief physician at the Court of King Louis the XIVth of France. Of course. It was all coming back to me now. His word in diagnoses and treatment was law at Court. He used three main tools in treating his patients, bleeding them, purging them, and feeding them an emetic. He had a kindly bedside manner, all right, and an unshakable faith in his own medical acumen, so it never occurred to him that his methods were largely responsible for so many of his patients' deaths.

I was stunned. How did all this come to my mind? I was never a good English history student, and had not concerned myself with the French at all.

"*Enchanté de vous revoir, mon ami,*" he said bowing ceremoniously and as he did so, the crisp bib he wore crinkled and pressed against his chin, creating pitted folds on his already odious face. To my amazement, I understood every word of his impeccable French greeting although the extent of my knowledge of French was limited to abortive efforts in my college years. I was even more surprised to hear myself responding to Monsieur Fagon in the flowery sentences of his times. *"Le plaisir est tout à moi, Monsieur,"* I said bowing back.

"I never thought you would follow in Mareschal's footsteps," Fagon said with a tinge of contempt in his voice. "You never had much respect for his skills."

"With Monsieur Fagon's permission, I would like to correct that impression. I had profound respect for Mareschal's skills as a surgeon. My only doubts were in regard to his intellectual perspicacity."

I bowed to Fagon again and bit my lip trying hard not to laugh. The formality of my speech amused me. I knew that my name was James Braddock and that I belonged to the twentieth century, but although I could not remember all the details of my life as a Frenchman, I knew exactly to what Fagon was referring.

It seemed that after all this time he was still resentful of the fact that while he treated the dying king for sciatica, it was Mareschal, the court surgeon, called in for consultation a few days later, who correctly diagnosed a gangrenous leg and suggested its amputation. Fagon was horrified and dismissed the surgeon with a wave of his hand. A few days later, it was too late to save the king.

I could not remember any subsequent events or my own part in the drama, but every indirect reference to a particular episode triggered the scene in careful detail. Although I wanted to talk to Fagon, I became aware of a putrid odor around him that was sickening. I moved away.

When I turned to rejoin Professor Farnsworth, I nearly walked into the floor length mirror in a gold-leaf frame hanging between rows of chairs. This time I saw my reflection in it well-defined, still wearing the navy blue blazer and gray slacks I had put on that Saturday morning. Reassured by the image, I nevertheless stared at myself in disbelief. Somewhat thinner, with the waistline trim, my posture erect, (I have been slipping into a tired slouch lately) my body was now youthful. But that wasn't all. My eyes shone with vigor, the tired pouches under them were gone, and my sallow face had gained color and softened the sagging jowls of middle age.

Delighted with what I saw, my glance fell on a young woman standing quietly in a shadow somewhat apart from the rest of the group. She was dressed in a red costume with a short train to her skirt, an embroidered tunic that nipped at the waist and flared at the hips, and a lace bow under her rounded chin that softened the severity of a high stiff collar. In her left hand she held a lace handkerchief.

Although she presented an exquisite picture of grace and beauty, it was something else that made my heart turn over. With unshakable awareness I knew that I had loved this woman and she belonged to me in France. I was transfixed. I wanted to touch her, to hold her in my arms.

She wore no wig and small wonder. Mounds of cascading flaxen curls tumbled down her shoulders, spilling over her forehead from under a black hat trimmed with white ostrich feathers. Because she stood in semi-darkness, I could not tell the color of her eyes, but the dewy texture of her skin glowed in the dim light accentuated by the softness of her parted lips and the oval contour of her face.

I dared not move. What if the spell was broken and she disappeared before I found out who she was? Our eyes locked and gradually the room and everyone in it receded, leaving us alone in a strange communion of silence. I had no doubt whatsoever that she had been mine, that a bond existed between us forged by a millennium of time which neither betrayal nor death could break, and that finally, she was one with me.

A glow appeared around her head and in the region of her heart. It quivered slightly with a bluish light, grew stronger, bursting forth to bathe her, then reaching out toward me until we were engulfed in it together. I was filled with a kind of joy and peace I had never known before. Everything trembled within me at a high pitch as if the trill of a musical instrument had struck a responding key in the nerves of my spine. I was filled with renewed energy which surged upward, first to my heart, making it pound in rhythmic cadence, and then filling my whole body, making me feel exhilarated, weightless.

To reach this woman in red, to hear her voice again—yes, I knew that I had heard it before—had become an overwhelming desire to the exclusion of anything else, for at that instant I realized that this woman was the same as the golden image I had seen when I first found myself in this dimension.

I made a move toward her and without thought, called, "Louise!"

I broke the spell. In a flash the light faded and with it the woman in red. As she disappeared behind the door, the floral scent of her perfume lingered in the room. I recognized it instantly, and knew at once that she had been my wife. We met in 1694, when she was eighteen and I was already thirty-three. She was so delicately beautiful as she curtseyed to the king that I fell in love with her on the spot. Daughter of a marquis, she was appointed as maid of honor to the king's sister-in-law, the Duchesse d'Orlèans, commonly addressed as Madame. We were married a year later over her parents' disapproval and the courtiers' raised brows because I came from minor nobility, and as a physician, was in the service to the king. But our mutual love prevailed and when her parents saw how much in love we were, they relented.

At first I worried about the king's notoriously roving eye, especially since he preferred blondes, and the beauty of Louise's flaxen hair was impossible to hide. Both of his favorites, Louise de la Vallière and Marquise de Montespan were blond. Fortunately, my Louise was never flirtatious and studiously avoided making direct eye contact with the king.

Although we were disappointed at not being blessed with children, our love deepened with every passing year. "How is it possible to love you even more today than I did yesterday?" I would say to her periodically and she would laugh and kiss me lightly on the cheek. We never quarreled and what disagreements we had were so minor that I could not remember them. When I once told her that I worshiped her, she grew serious and spoke so softly that I could barely hear her.

"In many ways, yes, *cheri*, except as an equal partner in life."

"What on earth do you mean, my love? You know how much I adore you."

"Perhaps there's the answer," she said wistfully. "Bring me down a little from that pedestal. You hold back. You don't share with me your thoughts and worries. You treat me like I'm not alive."

She left me standing in the middle of our bedchamber wondering if she suspected anything, for while my love grew, the passion I had felt for her in the beginning had waned with the passing years.

I was too busy, too selfish with my obligations to Fagon and the king to dwell on it then and dismissed her words as a childish whim of a pampered wife, who had always deferred to me on all my decisions and never questioned them.

Yes, I adored her. So much so, that when I made love to her, I venerated her body more than lusted for it. As for lust, I had a secret outlet, Madame la Comtesse de la Galère, one of the ladies at the Court, a fiery brunette with dark brown eyes that inflamed me every time I looked into them. It was a perfect arrangement for me, for I had two separate worlds, my goddess Louise, cherished and fiercely protected from any gossip, and the countess, whose vapid and ailing husband had turned a blind eye to his wife's indiscretions. Our affair was mutually agreeable with no strings attached. What more could I have wanted?

I chuckled at times when I thought that the king had a mistress by the name of Louise de La Vallière and mine was Comtesse de la Galère. It amused me to think that their names rhymed. It appealed to my sense of poetic justice -- if the king openly had mistresses, there was no reason why we at Court shouldn't follow suit, except that mine was clandestine. Other wives accepted their husbands' infidelities as status quo, but in my case, I didn't want to destroy my angel's trust. Comtesse de la Galère sensed my fear of Court gossip and one day patted my arm. "Don't worry, cheri," she said with a twinkle in her eye. "I won't ever betray you. I don't speak of our relationship with anyone for the simple reason that I am in the same position as you are."

When I raised my brows, she went on, "I don't want my husband to find out about us either. He's been good to me and I don't want to hurt his feelings any more than you do to your Louise."

I was grateful to this voluptuous aristocrat who exuded such sexuality that I wondered how she ever agreed to marry her dull husband, a good twenty-five years her senior. But then arranged marriages for a variety of reasons were *de rigueur* at Court.

Dr. Farnsworth took my arm and brought me back to the present. "Sit down, Jim. You look dazed."

"I'm beginning to remember things..." I let the sentence hang for a moment and then said, "By the way, Fagon didn't react at all to my being dressed in my 20th century suit."

"He remembered you as his assistant at Court, so he saw you as you were in that era."

I sat facing Professor Farnsworth and tried to assimilate what he said but my mind wandered. I could absorb only a certain amount of information at once and too much had been thrown at me in too short a time. In the beginning I had clung to the illusion of being still in the physical world, but then I discovered that the astral plane was a more real existence for me. Here, I had no demoralizing reminders that I was different from others when I could walk through doors and remain invisible. For the moment, at least, I felt the comforting firmness of the silk damask upholstery and my feet rested solidly on the wood inlaid floor. If it weren't for the disconcerting way in which this unpredictable astral world surprised me with its seemingly supernatural feats of materializing my thoughts and projecting my emotions in a burst of light and moving shapes, I could, just possibly, begin to enjoy this new environment with my ability to create objects at will and move instantly from place to place. I could even have fun talking to these people from the eighteenth century and reliving my life with Louise, whom I had neglected far too often.

What fun I could have with Fagon, puncturing his inflated ego with modern science, making him admit once and for all that he was directly responsible for the change in the course of history of France. In short, he was a murderer without intent. Illustrious names poured forth flooding my brain. Louis XIVth; Monsieur le Dauphin, his gluttonous heir; his son, the Duc de Bourgogne and his wife, Marie-Adelaide – the merry favorite of the king with whom all of us at the Court were a little in love. All died while in Fagon's care. Marie-Adelaide's harmless frivolity brought a ray of sunshine to the Court's hypocritical piety enforced by the Sun King's favorite, Madame de Maintenon, or *Madame de Maintenant--Madame for the day*, as we all called her behind her back. How wrong we were! The King installed and dismissed his mistresses at will, even the *"Maitresse en Titre,"* the established favorites like Madame de la Vallière or Madame Montespan, and we all thought that Madame de Maintenon would be dismissed with time as all the others. Instead, in her quiet, pious way, she endured, and there were even strong rumors that the king had secretly married her.

Memories of that era surfaced in fragmentary scenes. Louise appeared in my mind's eye, and suddenly a clear image of the Russian Nadine superimposed on her delicate face. Apprehension and anxiety swept over me. Louise and Nadine. Of course. They were one and the same. What had I done to Louise to be denied fulfillment of my love for Nadine?

The sharp contours of the furniture began to blur, the light shifted its focus, undulating the room, fraying it at the edges, throwing me into space. And then, all at once, everything faded.

CHAPTER 6

A soft, yellow light suffused the room around me. I stood at the foot of a canopied bed holding onto a red brocaded curtain tied back by a gold tassel. The five-year old Dauphin, his little face bathed in tears, lay almost lost under the bed's heavy covers. I reeled from the stench of vomit that hung in the closed room. The air was stifling for the windows were shut tight to keep out the chill February air. Fagon had issued strict orders that the Dauphin should be kept out of any possible drafts. It would have been a terrible oversight if the experienced, respected court physician allowed the child's measles to be complicated by a cold.

I looked around the room. Several women clustered together in the far corner were fanning themselves with lace handkerchiefs, whispering and shaking their heads. The old *Sun King* was sitting on a settee, his head nodding, half-asleep. His skin was sallow and he looked exhausted, but no one dared suggest that he retire. I studied His Majesty with compassion. He was 73 years old and heavy from epicurean excesses – the intake capacity of his stomach was legendary. His bloated face and puffed pouches under his eyes made him look every inch the weary old man. Keeping vigil in the child's room, he had had no dinner today. He never questioned the authority of physicians and it never occurred to him to object to the doctor's decisions. In the years that I had been Fagon's assistant, I had never ceased to admire his ability to take charge in medical emergencies. The fact that he was treating the King or the heir to the throne never shook his self-confidence. When royalty was ill, Fagon became king.

We had been through several crises together, including the death of the King's son, the Grand Dauphin, from smallpox ten months earlier. Sad as it was to lose a man in his fiftieth year, the events of the last few days were so painful that we hardly spoke to each other as we went about our tasks, stunned and shocked by our failures in preventing the deaths of the king's grandson, the Duc de Bourgogne and his wife, Marie-Adelaide, from what appeared at first as a mild case of measles. Now, their older son, the five-year old Dauphin, had contracted the same illness and it looked as if he were going to join his parents. Many times I would have chosen a different method of treatment but I never questioned Fagon. It was unthinkable.

The curls of my wig tickled my temples. I pushed them back. One of the rings on my fingers got caught in the thick hair and I jerked my hand impatiently, nearly taking the whole wig with it. Beads of perspiration trickled down my jaw crawling slowly underneath my tight collar.

I gazed at the child. We had applied all the usual remedies, doubling the dose of emetic for good measure, purging and bleeding the little prince to no avail. I wondered if the spasmodic convulsions that were exhausting the Dauphin were not caused by the emetic. I dared not ask. Anxious from the nagging doubt, I looked away from the bed covers soaked with the child's sweat.

Little Louis thrashed and whimpered. I reached for his hand and stroked it gently. It was hot and damp. What are we going to tell the King? Throughout the day, His Majesty had asked only one question of us, "Any hope left, *Messieurs?*" And his concern for his great-grandson was all the more pathetic after the tragic loss of his son and grandson in the past few months. The King and Madame de Maintenon were still grieving over the death of his grandson's wife, Marie-Adelaide, who was the apple of the King's eye. And then the little Dauphin also fell ill.

The King never complained. It was his brother's widow, the old Bavarian Princess Palatinate, fat and disheveled, who had burst into the room earlier in the day and begged Fagon not to give the child any more emetic. I was shocked by her audacity in meddling in medicine and daring to tell Fagon what to do. But Fagon, unfailingly courteous, explained to Madame that since he could not leave the Dauphin's side to talk to her further, he would send me, his assistant, Etièn Louvois, to her apartments.

Now I shuddered at the memory of that visit. The Princess Palatinate had always intimidated me by her voluminous bulk, and her great size made my limited height all the more embarrassing.

She was a formidable woman. Outspoken and critical, she feared no one and frequently rocked the established conventions of the Court. Hating the confrontation and the Princess' sharp tongue which I expected to lash at me momentarily, I searched my clothing for a pocket comb with which to scratch on her door before entering. It had been eighteen years since I joined the Court, but I had never forgotten the admonishment I received for the breach of Court etiquette when I had knocked on the door with my hand. Most courtiers grew a long nail on the little finger for the purpose, and that is what I now used, failing to find the comb.

As I had feared, the Princess immediately rushed into a monologue on the evils of the emetic.

"Did it ever occur to you why the Dauphin is having convulsions?" she said. "There are no more fluids left in his body from all that poison you gave him. It's bad enough that you don't give him any fluids to drink, but you bleed him as well. Can't you speak up and make the King order Fagon to stop torturing the child?"

I bowed to her ceremoniously from the waist. "Madame," I said, "Monsieur Fagon has years of professional experience and he knows what he is doing. We have no right to question him. The emetic has valuable therapeutic value in ridding the body of poisons. It has been proven again and again as a safe and necessary treatment."

My words did not sound convincing. I resented having to defend our professional judgment to a woman, and one who knew so little of medical science, but there was another, more elusive reason. In the hidden chambers of my brain doubts lurked. Could she, this proud, opinionated woman who filled her days writing gossipy letters to her numerous relatives in Germany, possibly be right?

I returned to the sick chamber. The little Dauphin was vomiting again. So I walked around the foot of the bed and supported his forehead with the palm of my hand. Fagon was wheezing and mopping his own forehead with his handkerchief. I felt sorry for him. We were all under stress but his anxiety was complicated by asthma. The white lace of his cuff was stained with greenish vomitus of the child. Our eyes met and locked.

"The Dauphin is going to die." Fagon's voice was barely audible. "Go and find his little brother and see if he is well. If not, we might just get to him early enough to save him."

Fagon's eyes were bloodshot from lack of sleep as he looked around the room in search of someone.

"She is not here," he whispered.

"Who isn't here?" I asked.

"*Duchesse de Ventadour*, the second child's governess. Go, find her!"

There was urgency in his last words and, lowering the Dauphin's head on the pillow, I wiped his bluish lips with a towel and hurried out of the bedchamber. Strange, how in the urgency of one's quest, a few minutes seem to become hours. Every courtier I met in the endless row of parlors, antechambers and halls, shrugged his shoulders and pointed to the royal nursery which seemed farther and farther away as I ran toward it.

I crossed the polished floor of the last room before reaching the nursery, careful not to lose my footing on the slippery parquet, and called to *Duchesse de Ventadour*. Almost at once the door moved slightly ajar, and noiselessly, with only a swishing of her skirt, La Duchesse de Ventadour glided into the room, closing the door firmly behind her. I bowed formally, taking in her elegance as I did so. Her blue silk skirt was superimposed with horizontal stripes of darker blue velvet and the matching bodice was held by a tight row of silk bows, graded in size from her bosom to the tiny waist, accentuating a very shapely figure.

I cleared my throat. "Madame La Duchesse, Monsieur Fagon commissioned me to examine the child in your charge to see if he has not contracted the measles from his brother."

The duchess leaned against the gilded door and produced the prince's little jacket from behind her back. "The prince is in my own room, Monsieur. I took him out of his nursery."

"Why?"

"Because that's where the Dauphin became ill, and I wanted to protect his little brother from getting the measles if he stayed in the same room."

"May I go to your room then, Madame, and examine him there?"

"No, indeed, you may not, Monsieur. The prince is perfectly well, I can assure you."

"Then why are you reluctant to let me see him?"

The duchess remained silent for a moment, her large gray eyes burrowing into mine defiantly. When she spoke again, there was unmistakable sarcasm in her voice. "With Monsieur's kind permission, I would like to point out that a man of your esteemed profession has to agree that the risk of delayed treatment is less than the chance of contagion that you might bring on your person from the sickroom."

I flushed at the formal rebuke and bowed low to hide my embarrassment. "Madame," I said, "I cannot impress upon you enough the importance of notifying us immediately should the prince become ill."

The duchess acknowledged my words with a haughty nod and stood waiting for me to leave. I had no alternative but to bow my way out of the room. She was a proud woman and obviously determined to protect her charge. For the moment I could not force the issue and enter the room without a serious breach of etiquette. I knew the King abhorred even the slightest infraction upon the stringent Court protocol, and followed its elaborate rules to the letter. For instance, the King would be up for hours working on his state papers before the time of the formal ceremonial "lever" but still, he would rush back to his bedchamber and submit to a morning dressing ritual attended by the dignitaries of the court who vied for the honor of passing a piece of underwear to their royal charge.

I sighed. There was nothing for me to do but to return to the sickroom and see what else I could do to help Fagon in ministering to the dying child.

"Le Dauphin est mort!"

The courtier's voice proclaiming from the balcony of the palace the Dauphin's death sounded distant and hollow through the walls, but the mournful wail from the waiting crowd below was clear enough. With a trembling hand I reached for a chair behind me and sat down. God! In the last ten months we had lost three heirs to the throne.

Who next? I buried my face in my hands, rubbing my temples with my thumbs.

*   *   *

"Tired, *cheri?*"

I jumped. Louise. I would recognize that voice anywhere. Anytime. After sixteen years of marriage I still thrilled to the sound of it. Maybe because it was a childless union, our love grew to encompass parental shading, as though we, as lovers, also created a part of the other. I stood up and put my arms around her.

She felt feverish. I pushed her away and looked into her blue eyes anxiously. They sparkled with unhealthy light.

"Louise, have you been near the Dauphin in the past few days?" I asked.

She hesitated, and then said, "The other day, Madame de Ventadour sent some toys over to him with me."

"How long were you in the room?"

"No more than two minutes. I gave him the toys, he kissed me, and I left."

I felt a chill. A terrible thought seared my brain. No. My Louise would not get measles. She couldn't. Not my wife, the joy of my life. I put my hand on her forehead. It was hot.

Whenever fear threatened me, anger came with it. "Go to bed immediately," I ordered. "Stay in our apartments and don't leave them. I'll check on you as soon as I can get away from the Dauphin's autopsy."

Louise held my arm. "*Cheri,* did you know that the Dauphin's little brother, Louis, has been sick with measles for as long as the Dauphin?"

Instinctively, I glanced in the direction of the nursery that I had just left. Rage blinded me. "That--that hypocrite!"

"I don't know who you are talking about, *cheri*, but Madame de Ventadour has been caring for him all this time and he is better."

"Thank God that he has survived so far. No thanks to the folly of that stupid woman. Do you realize that because of her we may lose the last heir to the throne?"

In spite of my anger, I was aware that Louise was watching me closely. "*Cheri*, please don't be angry with me when I say this, but can't you admit the possibility that Madame de Ventadour actually saved the new Dauphin's life?"

I was incredulous. "Saved his life? How?"

"She brought in a wet nurse and put him back to breast-feeding. She also kept him warm and quiet."

"She must be insane. The child is too old for breast-feeding."

"I don't think so, *cheri*. He is only two years old and still a baby in many ways."

"Well, what else did she do, besides defy the doctors' orders?"

"She took him to her own room away from possible contagion and where he would not be disturbed by anyone." Louise hesitated for a moment. "Not only Madame de Ventadour, but many other ladies at the Court believe that bleeding and emetics weaken the body so much that the sick person has no resistance left and dies."

I frowned. "What you're saying is heresy. Those women are meddling in something they know nothing about. Surely *you* don't doubt Monsieur Fagon's years of experience?"

Louise answered with a question. "Could it be that Monsieur Fagon is using methods he has learned in school simply because they are time honored and not time proven? Doesn't it ever occur to him that his treatment may retard the cure and often hasten death?"

"So, those women have corrupted your thinking too."

"No, *cheri*." Louise's voice was gentle. "It was I who suggested to Madame de Ventadour that she rescue the last prince."

Shocked, I stared at her. Then fearful that in this gossip-drowned palace at any moment someone might overhear us and report Louise to the King, I pushed her quickly toward the door. "The important thing for you to do, Louise, is to be in bed and rest so that you may be free of your fever."

At the door Louise paused and turned to face me. Two red spots burned on her cheeks and her luminous eyes shone brightly.

"*Cheri!*" Her voice was low but clear. "I shall do as you say, but only because it is you. Don't send Monsieur Fagon to see me if you don't want to be embarrassed. I will not allow him to enter our bedchamber."

There was a quiet finality in Louise's voice that made me realize that her determination was not caused by an emotional outburst of a feverish mind, but was born of gradual conviction.

Taken aback by the discovery that Louise had a mind of her own and a strong will in denying Fagon access to our bedchamber, I suddenly felt faint with tiredness. I sank into a chair behind me and buried my face in my hands.

Louise.

*   *   *

When at length I opened my eyes again, I couldn't calculate the passage of time, although I sensed that a few years had passed, for I stood once again at the foot of a canopied bed, this time adorned with white plumes behind a balustrade of carved and gilded wood. His face bathed in perspiration, the Sun King himself was lying on the bed stoically enduring obvious pain. I could see one of his legs, swollen and gangrenous, submerged in a bucket of red wine. In spite of the pots of jasmine that the King liked to crowd into his bedchamber, the air was pregnant with the odors of sour wine, stale breath, and festering gangrene.

Straining my mind, I tried to remember what had happened since Louise had left the room. Flashes of scenes, fragmentary phrases, descended upon me from all sides.

Louise in bed with measles. Thrashing, burning with growing fever. Delirious, and because of that, submissive to my care. But my confidence, clouded by my fear for her life, faltered. I lacked courage to trust my own judgment. In my medical studies we students were warned over and over not to treat members of our own family for that very reason. Desperate, I broke my promise to Louise and called in Fagon. I justified my action by convincing myself that she was already delirious and wouldn't know that Fagon was taking over. Such was my training of obedience to Fagon that, distraught, I followed his orders without question,'give her another emetic...bleed her from her left ankle...keep all the windows closed...make her perspire...'

Deprived of sober thought, I shunned common sense which had served me well in the past. Still, it continued to needle my brain without mercy. *If four people had died from measles in spite of Fagon's treatment, then...* I left the thought unfinished, moving about like a puppet, depending upon this man to save my wife.

The day before she died, Louise regained consciousness. She recognized Fagon and asked to speak to me alone. After keeping a sleepless vigil in our bedchamber for two days, I had escaped to the *Comtesse de la Galère's* apartments for a few hours, and that is where the messenger found me.

I hurried to Louise's bedside full of hope that perhaps the fever had broken and she was on her way to recovery.

For the rest of my life I was to be pursued by the look in her eyes when I entered the bedchamber.

"Darling," I blurted out, "I couldn't trust myself. I had to call in Fagon. Forgive me, my love, but I--"

She wouldn't let me finish my rush of words. My gentle, polite

Louise, raised her trembling, translucent hand to silence me, and said in a harsh voice, "Stop, Etièn. Stop it!"

Never had she called me by my name. It had always been `cheri' or `mon amour'. I knelt by her bed, tried to take her hand but she pulled it away and asked in a flat voice, "Where... where were you just now? In *Comtesse de la Galére's* apartment?"

I thought my heart had stopped beating, so horrified I was by her words. I could neither answer nor move.

"I had known..." she went on with an effort. "This palace gossip... reached me..." She paused, struggling for breath. "I wanted to tell you... that I knew... but I was afraid...afraid that if I told you, you wouldn't stop seeing her...and that would be worse." Her eyes filled with tears. "You broke my heart."

I seized her hands and showered them with kisses. "You are my only love, my soul, my heart." I could neither admit nor deny my affair with the countess.

With an effort, Louise pulled her hands away. "And now you broke your promise... you called in Monsieur Fagon. Another betrayal." She looked at me with eyes so full of pain, that I lowered mine.

"He will kill me...you know that. Then you and Madame de la Galère can...."

"No!" The strangled cry was wrenched from my soul. "Louise, forgive me! Get well. Live!"

She would not answer. She turned her head away and murmured something incoherent. Then with a deep sigh she slipped into a coma. I stayed by her bedside, held her hand, stroked her face, and whispered endearments. I hoped that she would regain consciousness once more, hear my plea and forgive me.

Fagon was long gone, leaving the servants to help me, but I sent them away. As the night approached I smoothed Louise's flaxen hair and touched her forehead. It was cool and damp. I pressed my ear to her chest. The heart beat faintly, irregularly. I placed my head next to hers on the pillow.

The gold encrusted clock on the mantel ticked the seconds, minutes, hours away. The candles in the wall sconces flickered, causing shadows in the bedchamber to move in silent grief.

Dawn had melted the darkness when the first rays of sun woke me with a start. I must have dozed off, and when I felt her hand again, it was cold. Fate deprived me of her last moments, her final breath. I wept over her body as much for her as for my guilt that overwhelmed me. Without any word of forgiveness, she died. Perhaps that was the worst of all. And her final accusation bore into me like a knife. How well did I really know my beloved wife? Too late I realized that I treated her as my goddess, pampered, loved, but never treated as an equal, never sharing my thoughts, my concerns, never asking her for advice, or giving her a chance to express her opinions. I knelt by her bed for a long time, over and over begging her forgiveness in futile hope that somehow she still could hear me.

*   *   *

On that day, I ended my affair with the countess. Too late, my conscience pursued me. And when at long last I allowed myself the luxury of thought, doubts began to assail me. Madame de Ventadour's little charge was the only survivor of the epidemic. But he was also the only one who had not been given over to Fagon's predictable remedies. My faith in Monsieur Fagon foundered this time. Too late, I saw him for what he was – a proud, narcissistic man limited in vision by self-aggrandizement, threatened by change and progress.

My memory, now honed by sharp recall, I looked at the suffering King with pity. Fagon, the all-powerful physician, the self-deluding, self-serving Lucifer was bending over the bed, the surgeon Mareschal hovering close behind. The king's thick black curls piled high on top of his head were parted in the middle into two mounds exposing a moist forehead. .

The King's breathing was labored but no sound of complaint escaped his lips as Fagon, with the surgeon Mareschal's help carefully lifted the afflicted leg out of the wine bath. The engorged leg was taut, glistening with dripping wine as though bathed in its own blood. The soaked red bandages sloughed off the oozing sores and hung dripping over the clean sheet that I had placed under it only moments earlier. Fagon, Mareschal and four other assistants bent over and busied themselves over it, shoving and pushing one another in their sedulous zeal like a clump of hungry maggots.

I stood aside holding fresh linens and watched the useless procedure of changing the dressings on the sick old man, astounded by his endurance of the torture inflicted upon him. At a loss how to help our august patient, we nevertheless refused to risk trying a new medicine offered by that charlatan, Le Brun from Marseilles who seemed to appear at Versailles unbidden with some obscure herbal mixture. Not content to abide by our decision, he influenced the Duc d'Orléans and other Princes of the Blood to allow him near our royal charge. In the end his ministrations failed to cure the King and Le Brun fled from the Palace terrified by our threats of prosecution for giving the King an unknown remedy. I thought of the king's wife, Queen Marie-Therese, who died from an abscess under her arm. She was only forty-five. Could she have survived if that abscess had been lanced? And would the king recover if Mareschal had his way and amputated the king's leg? The idea was abhorrent to me and I dismissed the dangerous thoughts.

Those around me were already mourning the King. I could hear the discreet whimpering of the duchesses from the adjacent study. Only Madame de Maintenon, the Black Widow, as I called her, for she always wore black, retained her ironclad composure, hidden and motionless in the alcove of the bedchamber.

I nursed my own private grief. Fagon was dead to me. And what was even worse, he may never have existed, not in terms that I had conjured him to be – wise, experienced, humanitarian. All this had been shattered when Louise died, but now even he had given way to fear. I had watched him as he stood meekly aside when Le Brun had forced his way to the King's bed.

The King moaned under the doctors' ministrations. Mareschal spoke soothingly to him. "Your Majesty has been so brave. A few more moments and it will all be over."

"Precisely," the King said. "It should have been all over last Wednesday as you had said, *Messieurs*... and here it is...what?... Saturday night?... and I'm still alive. At my age, I'd think... you could leave me to meet my Maker... without added delays. You know as well as I do... it's all useless."

The King touched his own abdomen. It was hard as a melon and glistened with perspiration in the candlelight. At last the men placed the re-bandaged leg on a pillow and bowed themselves out of the bedchamber. I was left behind to stand guard over the King's final hours. And they *were* his final hours, of that I had no doubt, for I had seen the increased swellings of his left side that crawled upward from his leg.

The Antoine brothers, the Grooms of the King's chamber, stood in the far corner of the room, no doubt ready to dress the King as soon as he died.

I squeezed the bedpost until my knuckles blanched. I felt ashamed of being a physician, of playing a part, however passive in this sham performance for the benefit of the living, particularly the new Regent, the *Duc d'Orléans*. It was important to Fagon and his assistants to ingratiate themselves, to save their own skins. Never mind that in the process they inflicted unnecessary pain upon the King, who they knew would be dead within hours. He no longer mattered. But what did matter, was to retain the continuity of their position as court physicians. Well, whatever the cost to me, I was not going to disturb the King during the night.

I only wanted to make his last hours as comfortable as possible. Stepping aside to let two men in black velvet habits pick up the royal chamber pot, I approached the King's bed. He was slipping into a coma.

"Your Majesty," I whispered, "you will feel better if you swallowed a few drops of this brandy." The King's eyelids fluttered but he didn't open his eyes.

I heard a voice behind me say, "Leave us, *Messieurs*, I wish to bid farewell to the King."

I turned around to meet the Black Widows' calm gaze. Her brown eyes betrayed no trace of tears and her folded hands were steady. It was rumored that she was the King's wife, and that he had married her in secret shortly after the queen's death. As we were obliged to treat her with great deference, I bowed and backed toward the door, but remained within view of the King, mindful of my orders not to leave him out of my sight.

Madame de Maintenon knelt by the bed and took the King's hand in hers. The King turned his head toward her and focused his eyes upon her face with difficulty. His voice was weak but clear.

"Madame, the only consolation I can give you is that considering our ages, this parting should not last long before we are reunited."

I smiled. I was sure that the Black Widow, in spite of her piety, did not cherish the idea of joining her husband in any great hurry. Madame de Maintenon rose from her knees, turned around and walked out of the chamber without glancing at me. I reached the side of the bed just in time to catch the King who seemed to be struggling to get up.

"Sire, you must remain in bed. Nothing will help your pain better than staying quiet and not tensing your muscles."

I tried to wipe the perspiration off his yellowed, shriveled forehead, but he pushed my hand away. Suddenly, looking straight ahead with unseeing eyes, he cried out, "Help, oh God, help me quickly!" Then he fell back on his pillow, and once more sank into a coma. He never spoke again. I stayed with him throughout the night and when the morning came with its faint early light and the room again had filled with people, the King breathed his last. I looked at the ornate clock on the mantle. It registered 8:45 in the morning. One of the Antoine brothers intoned,"*Le Roi est mort!* It is the morning of 1 September 1715." The other groom closed the Sun King's eyes and mouth and in the ensuing confusion, I slipped out of the bedchamber into the King's study. It was upholstered in green velvet and reflected the dignity of the King's office where he conducted affairs of state. From here I heard the Regent announce the King's death, and the steady mounting weeping of the women.

Fagon and his team would be preparing for the autopsy and I hoped that in the general confusion nobody would miss me. At all costs I wanted to avoid coming face to face with Fagon. I was no fool. I knew that I was fortunate to hold the position of assistant to Fagon, and to lose it through my righteous indignation would be folly. Yet, I wasn't sure that I could conceal my contempt for the man, or worse, force myself to offer him the obsequious praise he would expect for his heroic efforts to save the king.

Hypocrisy. Yes, the court was filled with it. It oozed from every pore, it permeated the apartments of the royalty, it contaminated the fetid air they breathed. Basic survival depended upon it. I felt unclean, oppressed, a pawn amidst the stagnant set of rules. For four years after Louise's death I had fought this inner battle of doubts and disillusionment and growing bitterness. The king's death had finally convinced me that Fagon's vanity and rigid egotism controlled him, and I wished never to see him again.

Members of the royal family, coming from their apartments in the south wing on their way to the King's bedchamber, passed through the study. They glanced curiously in my direction. I needed to be alone. So I walked through a number of salons toward *the Galerie des Glaces.* With everyone congregating in the King's private apartments on the east side of the Palace, I was reasonably sure I would not be disturbed here. I pushed through the richly carved and gilded doors and was immediately enveloped by the serenity of my favorite room. I walked slowly across the eighty yards of the *Galerie,* stepping reverently on the two *Savonnerie* carpets, which seemed as large as the meadows reflected in the seventeen arched mirrors that hung across from their corresponding windows.

The white damask curtains, the colored marble walls, the silver furniture – I looked at them all with a new, sharpened perception of a man condemned to farewells, to the last communion with opulence before the final exile. An exile that was self-imposed. Over the years since Louise's death, I never stopped grieving for her, never became entangled with another woman.

I made my choice. With a deep sigh I turned to leave the Palace forever.

CHAPTER 7

That was the last thing I remembered. Without awareness, without transition, I was back in the professor's home, sitting in the gilded chair. It was quiet in the room, and for me it was a time for reflection. Why, I wondered, did I relive those awful scenes? What was the connection between my lives in France, Russia, and the present? As I pondered them, a lot of things made sense. I loved Louise deeply, but I failed to see how intelligent and perceptive she was, and betrayed her with another woman. And so in my Russian life, when I was passionately in love with her as my sibling, Nadine, I could not have her.

Cause and effect. And now I had lost her until some future time.

But what of the *Comtesse de la Galère?* Who was she in the course of my relationships? And as I thought about it, my heart quickened at sudden recognition. *Comtesse de la Galère* was Irene whom I abandoned in Russia, and in my present life...could she be Gretchen? All the pieces were falling into place in my mind. Gretchen was getting even with me for my neglect of her in Russia. Would I survive this out of body experience to start over with Gretchen and wipe out the karma I had created in my past lives, or was it too late? And what about Louise-Nadine, the love that transcended two lifetimes? Where was she? The pain of that loss would not go away. I sat there hurting and going over what I had figured out and wondering if I was right.

The medical side of my life at the court of Louis XIV was abysmal. Obviously, I had been appalled by the lack of surgical skill and treatment methods of that day and I needed to see it to understand why I turned to surgery in this life.

Professor Farnsworth appeared by my side and put his hand on my shoulder. "Jim, you're beginning to figure things out for yourself. I'm glad. The learning process may be painful, but satisfying, isn't it?"

"What happened to me later in that life, Professor? How did I end up?"

"You left the Court and entered a monastery where you were able to experiment with your medical ideas more freely."

My anxiety wouldn't leave me. "What happened later in that Russian life?"

"You'll relive an episode out of that life that will answer many of your questions."

I thought of the professor's words. How far does one's tolerance have to stretch? I shifted in the chair and thought of the present life I had just left. Gretchen. Good mother and caring wife. She did seem to be interested in my work and delighted with my achievements. But she also wanted fun, sexual fulfillment, and when I failed her, she struck out at me in the way she knew would hurt the most.

I winced at the memory. It seemed so far away and yet so clear in my mind. The rolling hills of Heidelberg, the short distance vistas of the narrow Neckar Valley, the bustling cobblestoned streets, narrow and twisting, our house high on the hill, the beauty of that medieval town. We were each so busy with our duties. Gretchen – with social life – frequent dinner parties at which she excelled, always a new menu, an enjoyable group of people. I seemed to be on the periphery of it all, constantly planning another lecture, writing yet another article for the surgical journals, never sharing my concerns with her, or wanting her advice, yet acquiescing to all of Gretchen's social plans. I guess my disinterest in her daily life was transparent and even when she flirted with other men I was actually proud of her popularity and never stopped to wonder why she seemed so restless when I came home exhausted from my work.

She had already revealed to me the passionate side of her nature that both shocked and delighted me, but it had never occurred to me that those occasional interludes were not enough for her, that where I failed to satisfy her intellectual needs, she transmuted them into more frequent and physical experiences.

I remembered how at the end of a particularly successful party, Gretchen would often run into my den where I would be trying to catch up on my office work, and she, radiant with excitement, her green eyes sparkling, would clap her hands like a small child and ask, "Darling, wasn't that a great party? What did you think of it?"

With my thoughts miles away, I would glance at her quickly and mumble, "Sure, sure, great party."

I could see her shoulders droop and her face close down with hurt, before she walked out of the room, her enthusiasm punctured and deflated. But I was too busy to give it any significance.

One night, as I tried to dismiss her with my usual "Yes, dear," remark, she stamped her foot and screamed at me.

"You don't even hear what I'm saying. Stop giving me the `Yes, dear' routine. You're so damn polite, it's sickening. Don't answer me if I bore you. At least that would be more honest."

I was so startled by her outburst that I dropped my pen and looked at her in amazement. Two red spots appeared on her neck and I could see her jugular vein beat a fast tempo. Her eyes blazed with anger. She made a mock curtsy.

"Pardon me, Your Majesty, for daring to disturb you with my insignificant successes." Her voice was oozing with sarcasm. Then just as quickly it shook with rage. "Damn your lectures! Damn your precious research! I tried to help you with your work, I was interested in it, I sympathized with your heavy load, but I guess I'm not smart enough for you, so you shut me out. Damn..." she choked back tears, "Damn your brain!" She turned and rushed out of the room, slamming the door.

I sat at my desk for quite a while, wondering whatever made me fall for this shallow, temperamental creature who never seemed to venture beyond the narrow frames of domesticity. Flighty and sexy, there was no depth to her. The gap in our interests was growing into a chasm. Her reading material was limited to the metaphysical nonsense and confessions magazines which she perused by the hour and I had to restrain myself from telling her that if she had spent as much time on good literature and current events as she did steeping herself in weird books and romantic trash, she would be less oversexed and more balanced. I thought at the time that I made a mistake in marrying her.

I made a mistake, all right, in failing to see that books alone do not fill an emotional void, and that I was as much to blame for her flightiness and restless search for fulfillment as she was in turning to another source. It was a desperate cry for attention and I failed to recognize it. I didn't see that there was far more to her than met the eye, and I was to blame for not paying more attention to her.

One incident, one glaring example of my neglect of her came to mind. But I could not bring myself to dwell on it for emotions were magnified in this out-of-body experience to the point where I wanted to wipe it out of my mind.

My thoughts turned to Steve. Whenever any unpleasantness occurred between me and Gretchen, I sought out my son. When he was old enough to learn, I had taken time to teach him how to ride a bicycle so he could acquire a measure of independence from me. But he demanded more of my time than I had to give. How I wished now that I had made time to spend with Steve for although our moments together were infrequent, we seemed to be working on the same wave length. I thought of the day when I had helped him with his first science project in middle school. At that time he had asked me if it were possible for me to get a skull of a dog for his science fair exhibit and I had promised to work with him the following Sunday.

That afternoon, Gretchen and I had an argument – one of those inane sententious quarrels we were given to in moments of frustration. I was reading the New England Medical Journal when she entered the study waving a pair of my socks in the air. "When are you going to learn not to turn one of your socks inside out when you take them off?"

I hated to be interrupted while I was reading, especially a medical article. "For heaven's sake, Gretchen, can't you see I'm reading? Can't this wait until later?"

She placed one hand on her hip and continued to wave the sock with another. "And just when is the good time to talk to you?"

"Don't be sarcastic. It doesn't become you."

"I'm not being sarcastic. You're either on the phone with the hospital, or reading your damn journals, or watching the news on TV."

There were tears in her eyes that belied the belligerent tone of her voice. I knew that she was using the sock complaint as an excuse to draw my attention to herself and engage me in some silly conversation.

"Well," I retorted, "I certainly don't think a sock turned inside out is important enough for you to interrupt me."

"You're too lazy to take your sock off properly and there is something wrong with your brain if you turn it inside out only off one foot."

"You're being insulting. The trouble with you is that if you paid more attention to reading a good book instead of nagging me about a stupid thing like a sock, we would all be a hell of a lot happier."

We kept going on at each other and were so absorbed in self-serving rhetoric, that neither of us took notice of our child until he tiptoed out of the room. I stopped in mid-sentence.

I dropped the dead-end argument and followed Steve to his room. He brought home from school his science project and we worked on it for the rest of the afternoon, heads together, hands cooperating. His fingers—a child's slender, curious helpers—probed into the skull's orifices, and stroked the polished bone with a tentative touch. As we proceeded, it was uncanny how Steve anticipated my instructions of where to attach the threads from the various skull bones to the identifying chart.

"This is the cranium, right Dad?" he asked at one point and pulled the thread in the right direction. "And this is where the eyes were," he continued, rotating his finger in the empty sockets, this time with more assurance. Then, pointing to the back, forehead and ear area of the skull, he recited, "Occipital, frontal, temporal bone." I nodded, impressed by my eleven-year olds knowledge of anatomy.

"Great, son," I said stroking his head. "Are you enjoying this?"

He hesitated a moment, then looked up at me with trusting eyes. "I'm not sure, Dad. It's a bit scary."

"You'll get used to it soon enough. The more you learn, the more interesting it will become. Trust me!"

Steve didn't answer and I had an uncomfortable moment wondering about his reaction, but dismissed it as a child's fear at the first encounter with a skull.

When the dinner time drew near and I steered him toward the

door, Steve paused, looked at me with his round pleading eyes and said quietly, "Please, Dad, don't have another fight with Mom."

Yes. How many times was I to hear that phrase from my son in subsequent years? I ignored his pleas and shoved aside the gentle scratching of conscience, replacing it with the pressing, more important matters in my life. After all, I was not lazy. I was a dedicated, earnest surgeon, good provider for my family. That's right. Always the science. Always the physical comforts. They were important. They were in fact, paramount.

What a farce. A shaky façade built on quicksand. Well, to hell with the Russian incarnation. I've seen enough of my past mistakes. I glanced across the table to where Professor Farnsworth was sitting.

"Professor, I would be quite content to remain in your home and not go through any more experiences for a while."

He put his hand on mine. "Your mind is too active not to be curious about what happened in your Russian life. As a matter of fact, it will clarify some of the disturbing aspects of your present life, in particular your resentment of a certain colleague of yours."

I felt my face flush with embarrassment. "How do you know about that, Professor? Is this the hell I have to descend into now?"

"No, Jim. The hell we live through is the one we create ourselves. As I said earlier, you will see what happened to you in Russia."

The professor's words sounded ominous and I didn't like their implication, but I had learned by now that I was powerless to fight against the unfamiliar currents in the astral world. I walked outside and braced myself for the ordeal.

A delicate, transparent haze gradually shrouded the splendor of the garden, then darkened, and I could no longer distinguish the sharp contours of the flowers and plants around me. The professor's voice faded and once again I was alone.

Idle solitude was not a condition I relished. In the company of

Professor Farnsworth, I was still Jim Braddock, but the instant I was left alone in a visual vacuum, doubts assailed me. Was I once again Etièn Louvois at the court of the Sun King? Or Count Paul Uvarov, that high-minded roué in Russia? I could vaguely identify myself with the former—at least he was a physician--and not at all with the latter. I was much more comfortable as Jim Braddock of the twentieth century.

But what was I to do while I waited to see if my colleagues in that emergency room were going to be successful in reviving me? So far, I'd been reliving my lives, learning of my errors without a chance to redeem myself. I wanted to do something constructive, to return to my physical body, be with my wife and son, start over again and be a husband and father first and a surgeon second.

A wave of depression swept over me, crushing me with its weight. For the first time I knew exactly the feeling my depressed patients described before I sent them to a psychiatrist. It took me by surprise. I was familiar with frustration, anger, a rebellion – but depressed?

It must have been an outside influence for I remembered Gretchen reading to me once a passage from one of her metaphysical books about depression and how it influences other people:*Unlike a physical ailment confined to the body, depression affects adversely those who come into contact with the afflicted. The depressive vibrations fill the atmosphere and float in the air like leeches, waiting to attach themselves to whoever comes near them.*

I must have stumbled into such an area. Stumbled, or was deliberately placed there to walk once again through the corridors of time.

The haze lifted slowly and I was caught in a vortex of dizziness.

CHAPTER 8

I put my left hand behind me hoping to abort the tumbling sensation, and to my vast relief grabbed a hard object. It was a railing of some sort, cold to the touch. I hugged it with my left arm and with my right searched underneath. I felt a rounded column and knew that I was standing against a low fence of some kind. The lights in front of my eyes stopped flickering and I found myself in daylight. I looked around and saw water nearby. It reflected the sun and shimmered with ripples behind some floating swans. I was leaning against the marble balustrade of a gazebo that was perched on a knoll. I gazed at the pond. Its waters were placid, its edges fringed with giant ferns. A few clumps of water lilies hugged the shore, hiding from the sun's burning touch under the lace of the weeping willows that rimmed the pond, their delicate branches casting slim shadows on the water, brushing the lilies with a feathery touch. To the right of them the trunks of three birches stood out of the verdant foliage like pillars of snow. A black swan floated past me, his neck arched, his regal head motionless.

The air was scented like an aged wine—fragrant and heady and in the stillness around me, I heard no sound. Soothed, I sat on the railing and leaned against the pillar behind me, letting my eyes drift with the swan. Words and sounds knocked at my brain but I didn't react.

A healing languor came over me, guarding my mind from intrusive thought. Then I heard the call of a robin, persistent, reminding...

Memory stabbed me like a dagger, and the pain was physical. I leaned forward, clutching my arms across my chest and rocking back and forth to numb the ache.

Nadine.

The soul of my soul. My beloved sister. My soul-mate. Why did you have to die? You've taken a part of me with you, torn my heart out of my chest, left it hollow. I don't want to survive without you. Even here, in my favorite home. I feel your presence. You too, loved *Otradnoye*.

I held my breath listening. Not a sound. Stillness again. This *Otradnoye*, this Joyous Place we had called it, my parents' estate on the outskirts of Moscow, which I had inherited and which both Nadine and I had loved so much. A house of happy childhood memories was the place Nadine had chosen to come to live out her last days. She knew she was dying although her doctors insisted that had she gone south where the climate and the high altitude of the Caucasus were beneficial, she could have recovered. Nadine, however, had no illusions about her health.

When her illness had manifested itself with a dry cough, temperature that made her cheeks flame with unhealthy color, we both searched through every medical publication we could get our hands on, wading through Latin and Greek terminology, guessing here, deducing there, all the while hoping that a new cure would be found. Oh, the magazines were full of praises for Carl Joseph Eberth in distant Germany for his discovery of the bacteria that caused typhoid. They talked of Louis Pasteur working on lobar pneumonia in France. But nothing on consumption. Not one encouraging word.

The doctors were dedicated and hard-working, and they lectured Nadine who had lost her appetite, that a well-nourished body was better equipped to battle invading organisms. So intent were they upon finding a cure for the disease, so earnest in prescribing medicines to help the body, they never stopped to ponder something else.

The anguished spirit.

When doctors came to call, I would watch Nadine's expressive eyes. In the beginning I could see bewilderment that in time was replaced by fear, suspicion, and, finally, worst of all – resignation.

I tried the best I could to ease the hurt but I was no physician. I had no tools and no authority with which to calm Nadine's anxiety. I learned that death needs less preparation in the body but far more in the spirit. For through the spirit, the body can respond.

How I wished I were a physician! Perhaps I would not have been able to cure Nadine, but at least I would have better understood the process of her illness, could have given her greater support and maybe, just maybe, could have checked the burgeoning bitterness within me.

On that terrible day three weeks ago I had carried her in my arms onto our veranda. The morning sun of early September was gentle as I placed Nadine in the chaise-longue. Her hair had lost its luster, her cheeks were hollow and creamy-white with a shadow of death hovering near. We sat in silence for a while. I held her hand and kissed it on occasion, or rubbed it against my cheek, while she labored to breathe, to battle the draining cough.

I was grateful that the Preobrazhensky Guards required Nadine's husband to be present in St. Petersburg. I tolerated him, but felt he was a stranger, intruder into the bond that existed between my sister and me. I was aware that the link tying us together was about to be broken, and I fought for every precious minute that I could snatch from fate.

The servants had left a steaming samovar on the table with tea and cottage cheese turnovers that the cook knew were Nadine's favorites. I dismissed the hovering Nanny, electing to serve the tea myself, jealous of my privacy with Nadine. The tea was hot and in an effort to amuse her, I poured some liquid onto a saucer, held it on my fanned fingertips and blew on the tea to cool it, just as Nanny had always done. Nadine smiled. Encouraged, I laughed.

"Remember, how as children, we were punished for doing this? I can still see your governess, Mademoiselle Roget, clucking her tongue and saying, "*Quel mauvais ton, ma petite!*"

Poor Nanny. Bent over with rheumatism, half-blind, she had been a fixture in our home since the day I was born. She nursed me and then Nadine, and remained in our home ever since, even when her services were no longer needed. Proud and stubborn, she insisted on doing small chores like today, trying to pour the tea for us.

Nadine sighed, and looked at me, her eyes – two glowing gems in a withered face.

"Paul, I am going to leave you soon. I feel death approaching... but I must unburden myself to you." Her voice was weak and she gasped for air between sentences. When I protested, she raised her translucent hand to silence me.

"Please. I must. I *have* to tell you. I scolded you for your indiscretions. I made light of your special love for me... I closed my mind to the truth that screamed at me. This had to be... No other way was possible for us... But my heart knew. And knowing – ached. What is this curse between us, Paul? This bond I dare not name? It has shadowed both our lives... If God does not punish innocents, then why were we siblings?" She stifled a sob and gasped for air. "I have loved you always."

Her last words came out in a choked whisper and a single tear stole down her cheek. "Our church says this kind of love is sinful. But we broke no ecclesiastical law. We never sinned. We both fought against this power that held us in bondage... but was it really such a bondage?

I don't feel ashamed. I feel privileged to have had your love...and to have loved you..." A coughing spell silenced her for a few moments and then she went on. "There must be more to life than this short span. Surely this was a brief interlude in our eternity."

Words failed me as I wiped her moist forehead with my handkerchief.

She squeezed my hand gently. "Thank you, Paul, for not speaking. No words can describe our love...It is immortal." Nadine's labored breathing tired her and she paused again, dabbing her blood-stained handkerchief to her mouth.

I winced for her pain, but she smiled wanly and said, "You must fill the void in your life... Give happiness to others... Irene has been a widow now for several months. I am sure she still loves you. She is intelligent and she loves Russia...enrich your life... give her friendship and affection... marry her."

I longed to gather Nadine into my arms, to hold her tired body close to mine, to sustain her ebbing strength with the abundance of my energy, but all I dared was to stroke her hand, afraid to shatter the fragile moment.

A robin that had filled the morning air with a song, dropped down from a branch of an oak tree and perched on the arm of Nadine' chaise. It cocked its head at her and let forth with a low trilling sound. Nadine smiled and turned her head slowly toward the bird. Just as suddenly the robin took off and flew back to its tree. There it remained, silent, as if it sensed that the frayed thread that held Nadine's spirit to her body was about to break. Some believe that there is a strange affinity between animals and the dying. I felt Nadine's hand slacken in mine and when I looked at her, her eyes were half-closed and unseeing.

I made no move to release her hand. Her soul had flown, but her body was still warm and near me. I continued thieving from time the few minutes left to me with Nadine. After I called our servants, I went inside the house, afraid that my grief would defile the serenity of her passing.

Nadine's husband, Arkady Razin came down for the funeral. We had little to say to each other, and after it was over, he promptly returned to St. Petersburg. For days I was numb and when feeling returned, despair crawled over me, black, implacable.

At length, the day came when I realized that I had to get away from *Otradnoye* where every path, every bush, every tree reminded me of her. In the house it was worse. The old servants, red-eyed and sighing, tiptoed around, serving me in silence. Finally, I decided to return to St.Petersburg and ordered my trunks packed.

Once more I was drawn to the gazebo where, as children, Nadine and I played in the summer months. Surrounded once again by memories, I succumbed to a wave of grief that made me double over in pain.

Light footsteps on the gravel path, a rustling of skirts, and someone's hand on my shoulder disturbed my privacy. I straightened and turned around.

Irene stood before me.

I hadn't seen her since her husband's death and I was struck anew by her dark beauty. Her face shone with vitality and health and her brown eyes sparkled with warmth. Her hair reflected the hue of her black velvet dress.

"Paul, forgive me for this intrusion. I know you are in mourning and not receiving visitors, but I'm vacationing on my estate and when I was riding past your park today, I made my coachman stop, for I felt a need..." Irene waved her hand in search of a better word, "no, an urgency to see you and ask you to forgive me for the harsh words I used when I spoke to you at that last ball. I deeply regret what I said and have no excuse except to say I was jealous and that I still love you."Irene turned away and walked to the other side of the gazebo.

The black tulle that wrapped around the curved brim of her hat fluttered in the breeze sending a whiff of gardenia perfume my way. She turned to face me with a pleading look.

"Paul, please say something."

"Irene, it's all right. I'm sorry it worried you so long." I was startled by the hoarseness of my voice. After days of isolation, I found it difficult to speak. With an effort I forced myself to play the host. "Would you like some tea? The servants will be only too glad to—" Irene stopped me in mid-sentence. "Oh, Paul, this is not a social call. I came to ask forgiveness and, granted that, to make you an offer."

Crushed by sorrow, my mind moved slowly. "What offer?"

A fleeting smile touched her lips. "Before I answer, I would like to ask you another question. You retired from the Court after the Tsar's funeral six months ago. Do you ever plan to serve Alexander III or are you going to remain in seclusion, away from St. Petersburg?"

I knew that Irene was always interested in politics, but I was still surprised by her question.

"I'm disturbed by the new Tsar's repressive policies," I said. "I'll return to St. Petersburg, but I don't want to be involved in the government. We both wished for a constitutional monarchy and look what happened. Such a tragedy. I worry about the future. Sometimes I feel that we are sitting on a volcano whose eruption is long overdue." I gazed pensively into the distance. "I guess I'm too sad and depressed at the moment to make a final decision."

Irene moved closer to me and put her hand on my arm. "Paul, don't you think you'd feel better if during these trying times you were involved in our history making?"

I frowned at her. "If I proclaim my liberal ideas and speak up in favor of a constitution, the Tsar will accuse me of sedition and exile me to Siberia. No, Irene, there's nothing I can do."

"I know you too well, Paul, to believe that your conscience would let you stay passive."

She looked at me for a few moments, and then said, "Very well. Perhaps it was wrong of me to come here at a time like this. But it has to do with what I want to say next."

Irene lowered her eyes although she held her head high. Her voice was steady as she spoke. "Paul, I'm asking you to—to marry me."

Stunned, I took a step back, but she held up her hand. "Please hear me out. I have no illusions about your love for me. I know I could never replace Nadine in your heart, but I'm offering you affection, companionship, loyal support, and above all, a sharing of ideals and goals."

Unable to withstand my stare, Irene turned away and looked over the pond. I couldn't deny the allure of her warmth and sincerity. I felt a stirring in my veins. The past was irretrievable and my future loomed barren and lonely. Yet here stood a beautiful woman who loved me enough to offer herself in a one-sided relationship.

I heard Nadine's words again: *She still loves you. Enrich your life. Give her friendship and affection. Marry her.*

Nadine wished it too. I felt that fate was showing me a way to see a light in my future. I went up to Irene and touched her shoulders from behind. I could feel her tremble as she turned around to face me.

"Irene, I can't make any promises. But I'm willing to try. Give me a little more time."

She came into my arms easily and for the first time in several weeks I didn't feel so alone. She lifted her face to me and as I bent over to kiss her, Arkady Razin's voice jerked us apart.

"Well, well! I come home after a few weeks and what do I see? My Nadine can no longer satisfy your urges, so you lose no time in finding a substitute."

I whirled around. Intense loathing filled me with nausea. He never looked more repulsive to me than at that moment. So many years Nadine's senior, age had taken its toll, for his jowls had begun to sag, and his strong features were hardened by leathery skin. His deep-seated gray eyes now stared at me with unconcealed hate. I wondered how Nadine had tolerated him, even though she had married him because he was her first suitor and she knew that she would never love anyone else but me.

Out of the corner of my eye I saw Irene slip discreetly away and I remained alone with Razin. Rage welled within me. "How dare you! How dare you tarnish my sister's reputation? She's not here to defend herself!"

Arkady's lips curled. "Defend herself? For carrying on an affair with her own brother? I never knew of this until I found your letters to her a few days ago. I had to pull myself together before coming down here, and now this—this woman and you! How could you? You revolt me!"

"I will not dignify this with an answer. You"—I was choking—"you have a foul mind."

I started to leave the gazebo but he barred my way. "Not so fast. I'm not through with you."

He pulled an envelope from his breast pocket and waved it in the air. "There are two letters here. One is addressed to the Tzar detailing your incestuous affair with my wife, and the other contains instructions to you. If you ignore this second letter, I'll deliver the one to the Tzar myself."

"Bastard! You can't defame my sister's name," I shouted, "She's innocent! If not for the scandal it would create, I'd challenge you to a duel."

Razin smirked. "You don't deserve to die honorably. Read my instructions. The choice is yours."

He didn't hand me the letter. He threw it down at my feet, turned on his heel and stalked off.

At least he was giving me an alternative. I'd do anything to protect my angel from undeserved disgrace.

I bent down, picked up the envelope and in an instant found myself back in the same chair I had been sitting in Professor Farnsworth's garden.

"The letter!" I cried out. "Where's the letter? Professor? What was in that letter?"

"Easy, Jim, easy. You're out of Russia for the time being."

The professor's even voice did nothing to calm me. Disoriented, agitated, I leaned forward. "My God, Professor, a person can take just so much. Tell me what was in that letter!"

"I can't, Jim. If you were not given the chance to relive the rest of that life, then you were not yet ready to face the next scene."

He took me into a side lane shaded by plum trees and sat down on a bench. "Sit down, Jim, it is cooler out of the sun."

I tried to calm down, but the last scene in Russia would not fade away. "How does one control emotions in this discarnate state, Professor?"

"Look around, Jim. See the beauty around you."

I tried and gradually was able to understand what he was telling me. Near us on the Professor's terrace, were long baskets filled with tuberose begonias. I had never seen blossoms this large or the colors so intense. Fuchsias grew in profusion, festooned with their multicolored ballerina blossoms in varied combinations of white and pink and magenta. Spidery chrysanthemums, ivory-colored and full, were clustered nearby. I marveled that all of the flowers were blooming at once. A short distance away, a marble statue of Terpsichore sprayed water out of her fanned fingers, catching the sun in a prism of light.

Aside from the restful effect of the water cascading down like a myriad of sparkling gems, there was peace in the air and I felt surrounded by living, moving, breathing things.

I remembered now what some of my patients had said after they were revived during apparent clinical death. "There are no words in our vocabulary to adequately describe the vividness and beauty of what is on the other side," they had said.

Professor Farnsworth looked intently at me and smiled. "I can see that you've calmed down a bit."

"Yes, a little. But I have to know what was in that letter, and about the rest of my Russian life." I paused, and then swept my arm over his garden. "You're right. It's so peaceful here. Your flowers, shrubbery, trees, they are all healthy and fresh. Do they ever age, fade, turn color and die?"

"No, Jim. There's no aging here."

"In that case, you don't enjoy the changing seasons."

"On the contrary. You have only to make a wish it and it will appear before you."

I pondered the professor's words, awed by the limitless power of the mind. The light began to dawn in my head. "So. It's these emotions that play havoc with my mind. And I have already deduced that every experience I'm reliving has its definite purpose." For a few moments I was silent. Then I said, "I assume that the two lives I've just experienced are inter-connected."

The professor nodded.

"Yes," I said, "I'm beginning to understand. While Louise was alive, I treated her as a fragile Dresden figurine, an adornment to my life. I was heartbroken when she died, yet I never developed my relationship with her to any great depth. I betrayed her twice in France, but then in Russia I was thwarted in my love for Louise, who appeared as my sister, Nadine."

The emotional trauma I had just relived in that life was fresh in my mind and it still hurt deeply. "My sister..." I repeated. "My love for her was more than fraternal and I recognized it as such. What was in that letter?" I sighed and shook my head. "I see how I set myself back over the centuries. My lover in both lives was one and the same–Madame de la Galère and Irene and..." I caught my breath. *Of course. Gretchen... Passion but not a soul-mate. As Jim Braddock I wasgiven an opportunity to right the wrong but it is too late for me again, unless my colleagues manage to revive me. And how long can they keep me artificially alive before I become brain dead?*

Professor seemed to read my mind. "Time is relative over here. Remember, what may seem to you as a long time can actually be only a fraction of a minute."

He fell silent while I sat staring at the flowers before me. Their vibrant colors had suddenly lost their luster. "Professor," I finally said, "Isn't there anything redeeming in any of my lives to give me hope?"

"How about your dedication to your profession in the French incarnation? Think about it."

Little by little the jigsaw puzzle began to fall into place. "I suppose I've treated my patients with kindness and tried to heal their souls as well as their bodies. This time, of course, I have a better understanding of what it means to be a surgeon."

Professor Farnsworth turned on the bench to face me and asked, "What do *you* think you're still lacking?"

I thought for quite some time and then blurted out, "I guess it must be tolerance, but how far can tolerance stretch, Professor?"

He gave me a long, meaningful look. I squirmed under it.

"You mean Gretchen," I said, avoiding his gaze. "I can see now that I'm repeating my mistake by treating her as I did Irene in Russia -- a kind of sexual appendage to my life rather than loving her for herself."

"I'll draw you a parallel," Professor said quietly. "Tell me, in your present life, did you treat each of your patients as individual human beings or merely as subjects on whom to use your medical expertise?"

Dimly in the distance, a bothersome memory stirred. I closed my eyes to chase it away but it persisted. It was that day in San Francisco, the memory of which I wanted to suppress for so long. Two unrelated incidents took place on the same day. One was my discovery of Gretchen's hidden side, and the other happened in my office – a professional confrontation with a colleague over a patient stricken with terminal cancer. How did I behave in those particular instances and was that what the Professor was referring to now?

CHAPTER 9

I had been making rounds in the hospital since eight that Wednesday morning. By the time I got to the nurse's station to write my orders, it was ten o'clock and I was ready for my third cup of coffee. I knew I had been drinking too much of it lately, but the caffeine helped me get through the grueling day. I never scheduled surgery on Wednesdays in order to give myself a day to catch up on my medical journals and other paperwork. But since I was happiest with a scalpel in my hand, that was not my favorite day.

In the operating room I was relaxed, sure of my technical skill, in control of the staff and thoroughly familiar with the prone body before me. I had difficulty relating to the patient's need to ask numerous and frequently irrelevant questions. Surely my reputation spoke of my total dedication to medicine and constant search for further improvements in surgical techniques.

Their emotions disturbed me, and I fled their probing eyes under the pretext of an overloaded schedule. Usually I referred them to psychiatrists for a psychological crutch, thus avoiding responsibility that I knew was mine.

That particular morning I gratefully accepted the third cup of coffee from the receptionist at the desk. I had just checked on the sixteen-year old Johnny Williams who suffered from advanced

Hodgkin's disease and whose spleen I had removed a few days earlier. I knew that the boy was dying.

I was about to call his parents to get their consent to discontinue his life-sustaining drugs and let him expire peacefully, when a feisty nurse, Lucy Reardan, approached me.

Plump and short, no more than five feet three, she had huge hazel eyes that had a disconcerting way of looking at you as though peering at your innermost thoughts. She had specialized in the psychology of dying and proved of invaluable help on the terminal cancer ward.

"Dr.Braddock, I have just checked Johnny Williams. He is going to be a problem for a while. I only hope that chemotherapy keeps him alive for a bit longer."

"I see no reason to prolong his misery. All the tests show that the disease is so far advanced that chemotherapy is not arresting it."

Lucy's eyes flashed but she kept her voice calm. "That's just it, Dr. Braddock. He is physically miserable but psychologically he is not ready to die. I need more time to work with him."

"Is anyone ever truly ready to die? Certainly not the very young."

"In the sense you mean, Doctor, no. What I am talking about however, is his acceptance of death when death is inevitable. Johnny is starting to express his feelings about his illness and dying. He is so angry and bitter. I don't want him to die without a chance of working through these feelings."

"Those are noble emotions, Lucy, but we're here to heal bodies, not to practice religion."

Lucy pressed her lips tightly and I watched as she struggled to keep down her anger. "I'm not attempting to practice religion, Dr. Braddock." Her voice hardened. "But I would be failing in my job if I didn't do my best to help bring a measure of mental peace to the boy before he dies."

"And just how do you propose to accomplish this miracle?" I tried hard to keep sarcasm out of my voice.

Lucy ignored it. "Neither Johnny nor I can spare him a premature death. But I can help him reduce his emotional trauma so he'll be better able to accept his death. We can't deny him the time he needs. It's my job to see to it that he does. That's all."

I turned away from her and picked up Johnny's chart. It seemed foolish to prolong his suffering when medical science was helpless to do anything more than keep him breathing. Although my duty as a physician was to sustain life when there was the slightest glimmer of hope, in this case there was no hope of a remission, let alone cure. His latest lab work strongly indicated a secondary infection somewhere, often difficult to identify.

"Dr. Braddock," Lucy persisted, "All the signs point to his approaching death. A mini-extension, so to speak, is not going to substantially add to his suffering."

She joined her hands in a pleading gesture. "Please!"

Her rational arguments were making sense and I felt like an ogre. "O.K. Lucy," I said with a sigh, "you win. I suppose it won't hurt to continue the chemotherapy a while longer. Let's start him on antibiotics as well."

I scribbled the orders on Johnny's chart, handing them to her with one hand while trying to grab the sleeve of a passing colleague with the other without success. It was Tom Waverly, one of my former residents, now on the staff of the hospital. Tom, a thirty-nine year old bachelor, was an excellent surgeon. He exuded a health and vitality that all but pulsated from his six-foot-three frame. With his dark eyebrows and blue eyes, he looked more like a movie idol than a doctor. To me, his startling handsomeness appeared slightly effeminate but I could see where women adored him.

The day I introduced him to Gretchen I could sense the chemistry working between them. Over the months that followed, a number of incidents kept cropping up that could have been explained as circumstantial -- Gretchen not home on the same day as Tom was off; a day downtown described by Gretchen that Tom would mention at work; until one day I overheard two residents discussing Tom and Gretchen in a way that left no doubt as to what they were referring. I don't know what upset me most – the discovery of Gretchen's infidelity or the fact that she had become the subject of hallway gossip.

I didn't relish the confrontation with her and kept putting it off. Now, as I saw him rush past me, his coat tails flying, his surgical mask still hanging around his neck, I was surprised he was through surgery so early, for he was heavily scheduled for that day.

"Tom!" I called to him and he jerked his head in my direction.

"Oh, there you are! I was in such a hurry to find you, that I passed right by."

"What's up, Tom?"

"Your office or mine?"

Tom had a disconcerting way of coming straight to the point by omitting the preliminary amenities.

I shrugged. "Mine is closer."

Gretchen had just redecorated my office and although the cost had been staggering, I was very proud of it. I offered Tom a cup of coffee and pointed to one of the leather chairs near my desk. Tom however, refused my offer of coffee. His body was all sinew and muscle, and I automatically tightened my stomach, which daily seemed to inch its way forward. I wondered if he was still having sex with my wife, yet didn't want to confront him and admit to the knowledge that I was a cuckolded husband. Somehow it had been easier to close my eyes to the whole affair and pretend it was over.

Tom fidgeted in his chair, running his hand through his short dark hair which was beginning to be sprinkled with gray.

"What is it, Tom?" I asked tersely. "Out with it!"

"Damn it, Jim, where were you the last hour and a half? Emergency called and paged you but you didn't respond."

Surprised, I mentally reviewed the time. "I was right here, in the hospital, Tom, making rounds. I can't imagine not hearing the p.a. I'll have to check into that. I don't understand it, unless the paging system broke down on my floor."

"Well, it doesn't matter now. They brought in your patient, Mrs. Hudson, and I have never seen such a pathetic case in my life. I opened her up and closed without doing anything. The tumor, the size of a grapefruit, had metastasized everywhere. I talked to her briefly in the ER but she was wearing dark glasses, so not until I went over her chart that I saw what you had done to her eyes. God, Jim, was that necessary?"

I could feel a wave of color rise to my face.

Ginnie Hudson was a married woman of forty eight with a lump in her breast who had been referred to me by her internist two years earlier. When I examined her for the first time, the lump was already the size of a walnut and I had suspected cancer. My fears were confirmed. I performed a radical mastectomy but the cancerous cells had already spread to her lymph nodes. Subsequently, metastases had gone to her abdomen and brain, causing excruciating and ever increasing headaches. The pressure on her optic nerve was so great that she couldn't stand any appreciable amount of light.

The pain she suffered was difficult to describe. She was never still, going about her chores in her home, taking care of her family, moaning so quietly that it seemed that all of her strength had already been sapped by the consuming pain. Yet she continued to be up and about, dressed and her hair combed. I began to dread her visits to my office, for she invariably begged me to help her endure the pain, while refusing heavier narcotics because she wanted to remain alert.

She defied death by pretending to win the battle. Finally, I hit on the idea of easing external stress on her optic nerve by sewing her eyelids together, leaving only a small opening to prevent total blindness.

The memory of my dialogue with her husband made me wince. He was horrified. "Don't misunderstand me, doctor," he had said, pain written all over his drawn face. "I know you're trying to help her but won't this remove her from contact with the outside world?"

"She wants to ease the headaches, Mr. Hudson."

"That's beside the point, doctor. It's like..." he searched for the right words, "it's like placing my wife in a coffin before she is dead."

I was annoyed. "Do you want your wife to spend the rest of her days lying in bed doped with painkillers, unaware of her family around her?"

Mr. Hudson's tall lean frame was stooped, his face weary from weeks of stress. "You're brutal, doctor."

"Not at all. Your wife should be allowed to lead as normal a life as possible."

"But this is not a temporary measure, you're stitching her for the grave!"

I asked him to sit down. "Mr. Hudson," I said, "There are many other surgical procedures that change normal body functions so that a sick person can be helped to live more comfortably till the end."

Mr. Hudson winced. "Please, Dr. Braddock, spare me the details."

I put my hand on his arm. "My main concern at this point is to ease your wife's suffering and if I can achieve that, I'm sure she will avoid looking at herself in the mirror."

Mr. Hudson shifted uncomfortably in his chair. "Well, of course, her feelings are to be considered first. If she agrees to this procedure, then go ahead."

At the door, he paused. "How long do you think she has, doctor?"

I thought for a moment. "She is a fighter, so with intensive chemotherapy she may last for quite a few weeks."

Mr. Hudson started to say something but checked himself and left. I dismissed him from my mind as a selfish man concerned only with his own aesthetics. Then I called Ginnie. As I expected, she hesitated only a moment before agreeing. "Do anything, Dr. Braddock, to ease my headaches. Anything."

Pleased with the ingenious way I proposed to relieve her agony, I scheduled her for the procedure without delay. As I calculated, it indeed relieved her pain somewhat, although not enough without the additional help of dark glasses.

"Weren't the dark glasses enough without surgery?" Tom asked me now.

"I can assure you, Tom, I had no desire to mutilate her face, but she had gradually built up tolerance to narcotics."

Tom narrowed his eyes. "Evidently her pain was not confined to her head alone. She complained in the emergency room of stabbing pain in her abdomen. That's why I opened her up hoping against hope to relieve the pressure but I should have known better, I guess."

"Don't blame yourself, Tom. You were not familiar with the problem. I'm giving her an optimum chemotherapy regime and up till now she seemed to be holding her own."

Tom stared at me, surprise written all over his face. "Let me get this straight. With her eyes stitched forever, tumor pressing on her brain, another in her abdomen and metastases all over her body, you're giving her chemotherapy? What for?"

With unmistakable indignation in his voice, I found myself on the defensive. I wanted to explain my actions, the motivation which was not quite clear even to me.

"Tom, it's a bit complicated to delve into details. Haven't you read the latest literature on combined chemotherapy and radiation? They claim excellent results." Suddenly, I knew even as I spoke, that my words sounded lame.

"Of course I have, but that's beside the point. We are dealing here with a woman so invaded by malignancy that it would take a miracle to even cause a remission."

"But she's a remarkable patient," I persisted, irritated by what Tom was obviously leading up to – questioning my judgment. "Any other human being would have long been bedridden and semiconscious, but she is still up and about and fighting."

"And because she's still fighting, you're going to prolong her agony before you let her die?"

"Tom, aren't you being a bit melodramatic?"

"Hell, no. Temper your science with a bit of humanity, Jim. Are you trying to add her to your list of statistics? For Christ's sake, allow her the dignity of death!"

"I'm doing exactly what she wants."

Tom rose from his chair, leaned over my desk, and looking me straight in the eye spat out quietly, "Bullshit."

Then he stalked out of the room and slammed the door behind him.

I remained in my chair for a long time drinking my coffee. I felt stripped of pretenses by Tom's direct criticism but I couldn't bring myself to discontinue the chemotherapy. I didn't want to analyze the reasoning behind my decision and went about the business of the day without dwelling on the problem. A short time after that incident in my office, Tom died from injuries in a car crash, and I never got the chance to discuss the matter further with him. As it turned out, Ginnie Hudson died a few days later in spite of the continued treatment, and I was relieved of my nagging conscience.

*   *   *

Back with Professor Farnsworth, I tried to understand my motives. The professor narrowed his eyes. "Jim, I think you know the answers to those two incidents at the hospital."

I nodded slowly. There was nowhere to hide from the truth. I gave in to Lucy's pleas and Johnny died peacefully a week later, but I had no excuse for what I did to Ginnie Hudson. That was the hell over here – no way to atone for what I had done. How did I do such a thing, be all science and no heart? What possible excuse could I give the professor?

"That was a difficult day for me in more ways than one," I said more as a statement of fact than an apology.

"Yes, of course." The professor's voice was full of sympathy. "You were destined for a further shock that day, weren't you?"

I winced, trying to erase the memory of the painful episode to which he was undoubtedly referring, but instead, the shocking scene unfolded before me. I tried to think of other things but the past forced its way into my consciousness. I groaned and watched it as a silent bystander.

*   *   *

Later that same morning, having finished my work, I sat brooding about my confrontation with Tom, for once not enjoying my newly decorated office. Actually I didn't know who to thank for the comfort and the luxury of it – Gretchen or Heidi. The latter had left our household when Steve no longer needed a nanny, and gone into interior design after working her way through college. She and Gretchen remained fast friends. Heidi never married and was soon a successful partner in a small decorator's shop in the exclusive Jackson Square district of San Francisco. I suspected that it was Heidi who prompted Gretchen to pick out masculine, black leather chairs, Danish modern teak tables and subtle accents in brass. The sofa was upholstered in brown, white and charcoal plaid and above it in a teak frame, hung a sketch of a geometrical design done in ink.

I studied the room pensively, grateful to the two women for the distinctive and underplayed elegance. My thoughts centered on Gretchen. After the uneasiness I had felt in my conversation with Tom, not to mention my nurse Lucy's determined argument, I needed a change of scene. I was hoping that if not understanding, at least I could count on Gretchen's loyalty, and a feeling that someone close to me was on my side.

I checked my schedule. My office hours were not due to begin until two that afternoon. Usually, I spent the time between hospital rounds and office calls catching up on my medical journals and looking over my patients' charts. But that day I felt weary. I had a sudden urge to break my routine, to go home for lunch and clear my mental cobwebs. I needed a light touch. That was it. A light touch, and Gretchen could provide it. In a surge of excitement, I decided to surprise her. I knew she would be home as she too, adhered to a schedule and spent Wednesdays cleaning the house.

Feeling slightly guilty about running off in the middle of the day, I closed my office door, instructed my secretary to take calls until I returned, and sauntered out of the hospital afraid to look at the passing nurses, avoiding interruption, afraid that the fragile thread of my unaccountably giddy mood would break with the first intruder.

The morning haze had cleared and the city sparkled in the noon sun. The red cables of the Golden Gate Bridge towered over the rocky terrain of the Sausalito side of the span and the serpentine highway burrowed into the hill beyond. Emerging on the other side of the tunnel with the Angel Island on my right, I took the first exit to Sausalito. It had been a while since I stopped in that arty town, and the proliferation of shops that spilled all around the main street confused me at first, but soon I found the flower shop I was looking for. I picked out a large arrangement of red and white carnations, favorites of Gretchen, and placing the basket on a piece of newspaper on the back seat, hurried back onto the freeway.

Fifteen minutes later I was pulling into our driveway, disappointed to find a bright red Peugeot parked at the curb. The car was vaguely familiar, but I couldn't place its owner and the knowledge that a visitor was in the house stilled my buoyed spirits. I felt foolish coming in with a floral arrangement in my arms for no special occasion was imminent and I would be at a loss to explain my gesture. I decided to leave the flowers in the car and moved them into the space on the floor between the front and back seats. Then I went in.

It was very quiet. There was no one in the living room or the family room and the kitchen showed no signs of luncheon preparation. If the owner of the red Peugeot was visiting a neighbor, and Gretchen was alone in the house, I still couldn't believe that she would be taking a nap at such an early hour. Nevertheless, I instinctively tiptoed down the hall's tile floor toward our bedroom. The door was closed. That was strange. Having been raised in Germany on the principle that the more fresh air one had, the healthier one became, Gretchen always opened the doors in the house for air circulation.

As I stood wondering what to do next, a faint sound I could not readily identify came from inside the bedroom. I held my breath and listened. It was followed by a low moan.

Hot blood rushed to my head. I stealthily turned the knob, at once hating my surreptitiousness and yet wanting to enter unobserved. Propriety dictated my knocking on the door and alerting Gretchen and her lover. Her lover! Who could it be? Not Tom Waverly, for I had just left him at the hospital. Someone new? Anger welled up in me at the thought that I was so thoroughly duped that I couldn't even guess as to who it might be. Feeling like an intruder in my own home, I was overcome by desire to shame her. I threw open the door and walked in.

I don't know what I had expected to see, but nothing had prepared me for the scene before me. It had to have been a bad, sick dream. Not Gretchen. Not my wife. I blinked but it was not a dream. My throat tightened.

"Gretchen! Heidi!" My voice was hoarse.

They hadn't heard me. I couldn't believe it. I stood paralyzed as if in a nightmare watching the two women as they lay naked on our bed, disheveled and linked together.

The light darkened in front of my eyes but not before I saw Gretchen's face – her cat-like eyes half-closed and her lips parted in languid pleasure. Horrified at my own titillation, I heard myself scream, "Heidi, get out!"

I didn't trust myself to say anything else or remain in the room. Nausea rose choking me. I turned and stumbled to the bathroom. There, shutting the door behind me, I lowered myself on a stool, sickened.

I stayed there a long time, chasing away the sight of the two women entwined in bed. Finally, I pulled myself together and went to the family room where I could see through the big picture window that the red Peugeot was gone. I lowered myself heavily in my chair. I dreaded confronting Gretchen, seeing her embarrassment, listening to lies, accusations. But when she finally came into the room, her trim figure clad in a denim jump suit, I screamed at her.

"How could you!"

She covered her face with her hands and burst into tears. "I thought–I mean–" she sobbed, "I–I don't know how it happened."

"What do you mean, you don't know?"

"She–she was warm, gentle, loving–and she *listened* to me!"

"For heaven's sake, Gretchen, you're making no sense!"

"I–I need affection, love!"

"*That* kind of love? Is that what you call it? I call it perversion."

Her lips trembled. "I wouldn't call it that."

"Just what *would* you call it?"

Gretchen raised her head defiantly. "I think that none of this would have happened if..." she paused and sighed. "Ah, what's the use. You wouldn't understand."

"Are you trying to tell me that I don't satisfy you?"

"No, no...I mean yes, of course you do," she seemed to struggle for the right words, "but not often enough. If only you paid more attention to me...talked to me...*listened* to me!" She started to cry again. "Heidi made me forget everything. She–"

"Stop! Stop it this instant!" I shouted.

She hesitated, and then asked, "Do I shock you that much?"

"Call it whatever you want, but I have a definite word for women like you and Heidi."

"Oh Jim, please! I didn't plan this. It just happened."

"That's no excuse. What I saw was..." I paused to catch my breath. "My God, what kind of a woman *are* you? Tom Waverly and now Heidi."

She was silent for a few seconds, obviously surprised by my blurted words, and for a fleeting moment, I caught a look of guilt in her eyes.

"I'm sorry you found out about Tom," she said in a small voice, "but that's over now."

"No matter what you say, you can't undo what you've done."

Gretchen wiped her tears and when she looked at me again, her eyes flashed with anger. "What do you expect me to do, go down on my hands and knees and beg forgiveness?"

"This is getting us nowhere. You should be ashamed of what you've done, instead you're trying to turn it around and tell me it's my fault."

I could feel my voice rising but could not stop myself. "You waste your time on silly books, you show no interest in my work, and now you seek thrills with...with that woman!"

Gretchen's voice rose too. "Half the time you don't listen to what I say! You bury your face in your medical journals and pretend I don't exist. If only you paid more attention to me this wouldn't have happened."

"I simply don't care to continue this discussion any further. If you're to remain my wife, you're not to see Heidi again."

With that I turned and stalked out of the house.

*   *   *

As days stretched into weeks, I couldn't sort out my feelings nor bring myself to touch Gretchen. Our relationship became painful and distant, eroding into that superficial courtesy inherent in people to whom appearances are paramount.

I was painfully aware that Gretchen still had a powerful hold on my sexual drives and I coveted no other woman. We never discussed the Heidi incident again and by some power of self-delusion I convinced myself that it was a single interlude. She drew men like a magnet and flirted with them freely. As long as it was in my presence, I didn't mind it too much, but at times I felt her flirtations went too far and an argument would ensue. Gretchen never assured me of her faithfulness but rather turned the conversation around to accuse me of my indifference to her needs and to taunt me by calling me a medical robot. More and more I avoided these quarrels for they always ended with my feeling more the accused than the accuser.

In the dark corners of my soul, however, suspicion of her infidelity persisted. I hoped it would never surface and confront me again, but every time I ran into Tom Waverly at the hospital, a spark of anger ignited my fear of another betrayal until the tragic event that soon followed. As for Heidi, I had wiped her out of my mind until Professor Farnsworth triggered my memory and it came back in graphic detail.

In retrospect now, I could see the effects of my callous treatment of Irene in Russia reacting upon me through Gretchen.

Anger swept over me. I turned to Professor Farnsworth. "Why is it, that we are rewarded by such superb hindsight? Why things weren't made clear to me during my lifetime while there was still time to salvage my marriage? A lot of suffering could have been avoided if things could have been explained to me then."

I sighed and without waiting for an answer, looked around me, absorbing the peace and beauty of Professor Farnsworth's garden. "I think I need a rest, Professor. I would be quite happy to stay in your home here and not go through any more hell until I find out if they succeed in reviving me in that emergency room."

"Jim, while you wait, why not meet a few of your patients who have died while in your care?"

The professor's words did not sound comforting but I knew by now that it would be useless to argue. His voice receded, became garbled, and then mingled with other unidentified noises, hollow and distant. Slowly the scenery changed and to my utter surprise, I found myself on a ward of an unfamiliar, modern hospital.

CHAPTER 10

The first person I saw was Ginnie Hudson sitting next to her hospital bed. Her eyelids were still sewn shut. Without her dark glasses, the tiny holes in her lids were like gill slits. I was horrified. Under the pretext of my loyalty to the Hippocratic Oath I had prolonged her life at the expense of my patient's physical and psychological well-being. But in this astral existence, I couldn't understand why she still looked that way.

Instinctively, I set my neck deep into my shoulders trying to efface myself, to shrink my six-foot frame and make it unobtrusive. I couldn't face her. Not here, in this astral world, where emotions were rampant and guilt naked. I headed down the hall, away from her room. It was too late.

"Dr. Braddock!"

I stopped.

"Dr. Braddock, please! I need your help!"

What could I tell her? That I failed to apply the old cliché of tempering wisdom with mercy?

As I reached her, she grabbed me by the arm, clawing my sleeve in her semi-blindness. "Oh, please, you must help me find my dark glasses!"

I stared at her stupidly. "Dark glasses?"

"Yes, yes." Her speech was hurried. "I lost them and I don't want to leave the hospital until I have them. I don't want to scare people!" She smiled apologetically.

It was grotesque. She must have lost her mind. Unless...unless she wasn't aware that she had died. It was up to me to enlighten her. What would her reaction be when it all sinks in? I pulled her back to her bed, sat down beside her and told her. Her lips quivered, and then she sighed. "It's so different from what I expected. How stupid of me, I should have stumbled on the truth before this. What a relief that it's all over." Her brow furrowed. "Wait a minute! If that is so, then are you...?"

Two black pupils peered at me through tiny holes. They followed every move I made. I told her I had a heart attack and that I was not yet dead. She digested the news and then her voice, bewildered and preoccupied, cut into my thoughts. "If I'm dead, why are my eyes still stitched? Come to think of it, I just realized that my headaches are gone. Can you open my eyes for me now?"

Slowly understanding reached me. I could, and I would. But not in the way she thought. Not with a knife or scissors. There was an easier way, ever so much simpler and faster.

"You don't need the dark glasses anymore, Ginnie. And without any help from me, you can get your normal sight back. You said yourself that your headaches are gone, so you don't need your eyes stitched anymore."

"How can I do it myself without you cutting and removing the stitches?"

"By willing them to be open."

For a few moments she remained silent. Then, very quietly, she said, "I think I understand what you are saying Dr. Braddock."

"What do you say if we start by undoing what I've done to your eyes? Visualize yourself the way you were before the operation and make a strong wish to be that way again. The important thing is to put all your energy into your wish and not to doubt the outcome."

She turned her face away from me and I felt her grip tighten on my forearm. A few moments later she looked at me with her eyelids still stitched. "I can't do it!"

"Yes you can. Try again without hurrying. Calm your mind the best you can, and then try again. It may take several times, but you *will* succeed."

Sure enough, after a couple of more times, she let out a small cry. Large, curious brown eyes, lustrous from tears, looked up at me at close range with gratitude.

"How wonderful to have all my sight back! I feel like a newborn child who has to learn to walk and deal with the new world. It's hard to believe that I've died." Ginnie shook her head and sighed. "Strange, isn't it, how we struggle to preserve the image that we think others have of us, and then we fight to protect it at the expense of our integrity. How clear everything seems to me now. I see my whole life in an entirely new perspective. How much of it I've wasted."

"Nothing is ever wasted, Ginnie. Even the errors we make serve their purpose – we learn from them. Sooner or later we do learn. We mature." I ran my hand over my forehead. Yes, I thought, I have learned a lot in this dimension. "We do mature," I repeated.

"Not always, Dr. Braddock. I'm a little frightened. I don't know where to go or what to do. It's all such a surprise." She moaned. "Oh, and the regrets that fester in my soul! I'm so full of wasted energy."

"Here's the place to channel that energy into creative force, Ginnie," I said, fighting to control my voice. "You succeeded in restoring your lovely eyes, but you can also will yourself away from this hospital and to a place where someone will be waiting to help you adapt to your new life."

"Thank you, Dr. Braddock."

I watched her face radiate such joy that I smiled at her and turned to leave the hospital, but as I grasped the door handle, a hoarse whisper stopped me.

"Jim, remember me?"

Tom Waverly.

"You thought you would never see me again, didn't you, Jim?"

His voice jarred my thoughts, broke them up into a million sharp fragments, each one a painful memory. I raised my arm in lame protest but Tom ignored it. "I've been waiting for this moment a long time, Jim, going over and over in my mind what I would say to you and how I would get back at you." He shook his head with a bewildered look on his face. "Funny thing, now that the moment has come, I derive no pleasure in confronting you. I've spent the major part of my time in this hospital nursing my wound." He sounded bitter as he added, "My emotional wound, that is."

I thought of his last words. "You look healthy, why are you in this hospital?"

"My physical wounds healed almost immediately, but the miasma of hatred I felt upon realizing what you've done to me, keeps me chained to this place. I've been earthbound for a long time before I found myself in this hospital. Do you have any idea what it means to be earthbound, to hover near your house hating you, and following Gretchen around?"

My heart jumped at the mention of Gretchen. "I was there once when you made love to her," Tom went on. "The Church teaches us about hell and damnation and we create a remote fantasy, not unlike Dante's Inferno. I tell you, the real hell was in that room. There I stood, watching you and Gretchen together, hating what I saw and unable to leave. I still remember how I swore and pushed and pounded your bed with my fists without evoking any response from either of you."

A wave of hot blood flooded my face. The shame of this exposure was almost more than I could stand, but Tom stared past me with unseeing eyes. "Yes, that was the worst of it. This inability to touch anything physical. When I couldn't stand it any longer, I grabbed your arm but instead my fingernails dug into my own palm. I guess there is no greater hell than being earthbound. And the hell is twofold -- watching something you wish you weren't seeing and then, when the torture becomes too great and you want to interfere, no one pays the slightest attention to you because to them you're an empty spot. And then the realization comes to you that there is no bridge to let you go back. The finality of it all gradually sinks in, and when it does, you truly wish for oblivion." Tom threw his head back and laughed an arid laugh.

A chill went through me. I cleared my throat and tried to change the subject. "Tom, I hope you'll leave the hospital at once. It's not a happy place."

"What do *you* know about happiness? You rejected it when it was offered to you. You were incapable of giving it to Gretchen. She yearned for your warmth and clung to me only because she couldn't get it from you."

"Leave my wife out of this," I said, choking with anger. "You've done enough damage already!"

Tom laughed sarcastically. "You have the nerve to say that I did the damage? What about my car accident? Have you wiped it off your conscience completely?" A shiver went through me. I didn't want to talk about the accident, or even think about that day. Before, I always managed to suppress it. But now, it flashed before me in all its merciless detail.

"Your guess about my trauma was correct, Jim." Tom's uncanny timing in voicing my thoughts made me jump.

"As you surmised, I knocked myself out by hitting my head against the windshield. There was nothing wrong with your diagnosis. You were always an excellent diagnostician. But there was a lot wrong with your subsequent decision. No," Tom waved his arm impatiently to correct himself, "not even that. You knew very well what you had to do in this kind of emergency. But you wanted me to die."

I was furious. "You are questioning my medical judgment?"

"No. And therein lies the hypocrisy of it all. I could forgive an honest error. That happens to the best of us. But in your case you not only betrayed your Hippocratic Oath, but what was worse, you could not even be honest with yourself. And for that, I have not forgiven you."

"I don't understand what you mean, Tom."

"Don't you? You can't hide from the truth over here. That's the hell of it. You can't even kid yourself any more. How does it feel to be a murderer?"

"Just a minute, Tom! You're out of line. I did not murder you and you know it."

"What you did is tantamount to murder in my book."

"I–I hoped..."

I stumbled over words but Tom was relentless. "Yes? You hoped for what? For my death? There was a chance I could have been saved. But you made sure I wasn't. Like Pontius Pilate you washed your hands in righteous innocence. Only in your case, it was not innocence at all but a rather cunning scheme to get rid of a rival."

"I would never do such a thing. You're bitter...your thinking is clouded."

"Even here, when no pretenses are possible, you refuse to face yourself."

"Tom, that's enough. I'm not going to stand here and take your abuse any longer."

Tom smoothed the collar of his white sweater and chuckled. "Poor

Jim. If you only knew how pathetic you look." Suddenly his face twisted in anger. "You refuse to face it, and for that, I despise you."

"Tom, I won't listen to your insults."

"You're a coward!" With a sudden swing of his arm, Tom hit me across the face. There was something particularly demeaning in being hit with the back of the hand, as though he was sweeping me out of his way like so much dross.

I reeled and blacked out.

When I opened my eyes, I was lying on a bed in an elegantly furnished bedroom and Professor Farnsworth was bending over me. Then he pulled a chair up to the bed and sat down. With his chin resting in the palm of his hand, he watched me in silence.

I squirmed under his gaze. His gray eyes, clear and shining, seemed to see right through me. I had never felt so consummately exposed. In an effort to hide from those luminous eyes, my hand probed the surface of the bed looking for a blanket to cover my already clothed body.

Under his relentless scrutiny, I realized how ridiculous I must have looked – a grown man fully clothed lying on the bed and looking for a blanket. Without facing at him, I jumped off and rushed out of the bedroom into the large parlor where we had been before, then through the open French doors into the bright sunshine of his garden. I dreaded hearing his voice calling my name.

But silence prevailed like a protective shell. Afraid to trust my luck, I didn't pause to admire the beauty of his garden, but broke into a run down the gravel path, through the tall iron grill fence, across the open meadow and into the dense pine forest. I stopped when I no longer felt the pressure of the imaginary pursuit behind me and the shroud of fear lifted. I looked around.

I was surrounded by fragrant pines, fragrant beyond imagining. An occasional aspen brightened the darkness of the grove with the intensity of its golden autumn leaves. I was standing in a small clearing on the carpet of fresh grass. Unobserved, I sank down wearily on the ground and leaned against the trunk of the pine. I inhaled its fragrance, mixed with the pungency of resin, the same I had smelled as a child in the summer camp along the Russian River where I sat against a tree scraping the resin off the bark with my fingernails.

But now unaccountably, the pine scent had suddenly become unpleasant. I moved restlessly, reaching for support behind me, and as I did so, my hand came to rest on a live furry animal. I jerked my hand back and looked around. A russet cocker spaniel, his head between his paws, stared at me from below his brows. Relieved, I laughed softly at my own fear and stroked him on his silken head. Immediately, the dog inched his way forward without raising his head and soon was nuzzling against my thigh. In a few moments his paw was on my leg and before I could move, I was holding his warm body on my lap.

The sun's filtering rays probed between the pine boughs and the aspen foliage, dotting the grass with a yellow glow. The oblique shafts of light shrouded the clearing, slanting the air and reaching for me. I looked down at the dog, now peacefully dozing, and as I admired the shining bronze of its fur, a stab of pain hit my chest sending my heart into a pounding frenzy.

Tom Waverly had an identical cocker spaniel that died shortly after Tom.

I placed the dog on the ground, got up and walked briskly into the sunny haze. I didn't want to face Tom again. Not just yet. I glanced behind me. The dog was at my heels but there was no one else around. I looked down at the animal. He was watching me with plaintive eyes and as I tried to stare him down, he moved closer to my leg and rubbed his body against my calf.

I turned around and went back to the tree. On the grass again, I closed my eyes and put my hand over the dog's head while he rested his muzzle on my lap. I felt a measure of comfort from the warmth of his head. He cared. He liked me. They say dogs feel human emotions and react to them. Even if he were Tom's dog, he didn't seem to sense my involvement in Tom's death. My involvement!

Suddenly, I knew the reason for my shame. Tom Waverly. Of course. I had never admitted this to myself before. I squirmed on the grass, fighting the thought that would not go away.

"I'm not guilty. No. It wasn't my fault. It just happened before I could act."

The sound of my own voice stunned me. I sat up straight and motionless, my heart pounding. There came upon me a deep sadness of such weight and intensity that I groaned and dry sobs heaved in my chest.

There was no one around. To whom was I lying? Why kid myself any longer? How frightening it was to admit the truth. But I had to.

Tom was a good resident. One of the best I've ever had – smart, respectful and innovative. Just enough. He wasn't afraid to question, to speak his mind. I admired him for his integrity and singled him out as one who would become an outstanding surgeon, and I was proven right. I enjoyed his incisive mind, his curiosity, his sense of humor. Thus, when I overheard the conversation of two residents in the hallway of the hospital, it was particularly ironic that my star pupil had turned Judas.

Gretchen's betrayal was bad enough, but the humiliation of discovering that my subordinate was sleeping with my wife was the kind of indignity I could barely allow myself to think about. I could hardly stand being around Tom after that. A consuming shame became my constant companion.

I brooded over the future. I couldn't allow this to go on without confronting Gretchen soon, and trying to put an end to the affair. Undoubtedly, she would tell Tom that I knew. I would have to face him daily after that, not knowing if I was being duped on the sly again, being made a fool of, and wondering all the time how much he knew about my strained relationship with Gretchen. In that frame of mind, I continued seeing patients, doing my work mechanically, plagued by anger and hurt.

That day when the accident happened, the loudspeaker paged me and when I got to the emergency room, I found myself staring down at Tom's unconscious body before me. I was called upon to fight for the life of the very man whose betrayal I had discovered earlier. The ambulance attendants said that his car had gone off the road and hit a tree, but aside from a bruise on his forehead which might have accounted for his unconsciousness, I could see no other trauma to his body. On physical examination however, I realized immediately that his condition was far more serious than it had appeared at first glance. On his chest was a telltale mark of a steering wheel injury. I was reasonably sure that there was cardiac trauma with injury to the aorta.

An intern on duty stood by waiting for my orders. Mild excitement, like the rumblings of a distant thunder stirred within me. I began to issue orders for a number of tests and when I finished, the intern still stood with his pencil poised, waiting for further instructions. When none came, he hesitated, then asked, "Surgical prep, too?"

"No," I said. "Too risky to operate right now. Let's see what the tests show first. Then I'll decide."

But it was just as risky to wait. What I was really doing was buying time, not for his life, but for his death. I hoped the aorta would rupture while I waited and my conscience would be salved by the exercise of my caution.

The aorta had ruptured as they were lifting him onto the x-ray table, and the attendant ran out for help. There was nothing we could do, of course. I shut myself into my office, afraid that the enormous relief I felt might show on my face.

After Tom's death, I never revealed to Gretchen that I knew. I had killed Tom just as surely as if I had taken the knife and plunged it into his chest. Maybe he would have died anyway, but by delaying surgery I passed up the only chance he had of survival. I would never know whether it would have made any difference had I operated immediately. In either case, my guilt remained the same.

The dog whimpered and moved his head on my lap bringing renewed warmth to my chilled soul. To my surprise, I discovered that it was not as painful to admit an error and be repentant as it was to nurse my guilty conscience.

I dozed and when I opened my eyes, the dog had disappeared and I was alone again.

CHAPTER 11

Back in the professor's house, I stood in the parlor, uncertain which door to take to return to the bedroom where I had left him. He seemed so omniscient that I had no doubt he would sense my return. It wasn't long before I heard his voice behind me.

"Sit down, Jim. Perhaps now we can talk." He leaned forward with his forearms on his thighs, pensively studying his crisscrossed fingers.

I waited. The distant strains of Beethoven's Pastorale Symphony filtered through the open French doors and a thought came to me of how appropriately chosen was this piece of music for its sounds described the landscape I had just left. The trills were so real and three-dimensional that I could not separate the actual bird song from the woodwinds. Everything that surrounded the professor was in harmony, and studying his face I knew he was reading my thoughts. I held no resentment against it now.

"Loneliness is the saddest condition I know of, Professor," I said at length. "Especially when you're deprived of the one you love." My heart jumped. "What about Nadine, my Russian sister in the nineteenth century? I *have* to know! I want to see her. I want to talk to her as Jim Braddock and not as her Russian brother."

"You need not be so intense about it. All you have to do is look behind you."

I wheeled around to the sound of Nadine's voice. She stood before me in the same blue velvet riding habit I remember her wearing in *Otradnoye*. She seemed so real, so much flesh and blood as she leaned with one elbow on the ormolu covered wood desk, toying with her hat. As I made a step toward her, I turned back to make my apologies to the professor, but he was already gone. Nadine and I were alone.

I stood riveted to the floor, choked with emotion, uncertain, suddenly shy. Nadine moved toward me, a whimsical smile on her lips. Without taking her eyes off my face, she threw her hat sideways in a familiar gesture, and stretched her arms toward me.

"Paul, my love."

"I feel so awkward," I said, "not knowing who you really are, Nadine or Louise. You call me Paul and what shall I call you then, Nadine?"

"Names don't really matter. They change. It's the soul that remains the same. If you wish, you may call me Nadine. Perhaps it will be easier for you to identify me with that name."

I stood staring at her, trying and failing to sort out my feelings. To Jim Braddock, she was a stranger. A beautiful, warm woman from another era, a distant past. And yet, she was familiar, exuding closeness borne through years of mutual love, the kind of understanding that transcends words. I moved forward and at the touch of our hands, the barrier broke, doubts vanished, and I scooped her into my arms. She was not a phantom, but firm and warm and I held her close as if my arms could keep her forever fused to me, afraid to lose her again.

With my eyes closed, I squeezed her tighter, feeling her body against me, soft and yielding. I buried my face in her hair.

"My God, how I wanted you," I whispered. "I can hardly believe it. What happiness! Nadine, at last I can rightfully claim you for my own without fear of public condemnation, without feeling that this is a forbidden love, but best of all, I don't have to worry about losing you again. We've cheated death at last, darling."

I took a step back and held her at arm's length, looking at her, drinking in every familiar line of her face.

She took my face into her hands. Her blue eyes, clouded with sadness, stared back into mine in silence. The joy I had felt a moment ago snapped like a dry twig. I took her by the shoulders, squeezed hard. "Nadine, tell me I'm right, that nothing can separate us now or ever. Please tell me that!"

She closed her eyes and shook her head. When she looked at me again, two single tears fell on her velvet bodice. "Paul, my dearest, it's not yet time for us to be together. I'm here because I yearned to see you once more before..." She bit her lip and looked away.

I dropped my arms releasing her. "Am I forever destined to find you only to lose you again and again? What is this curse upon me?"

"No curse, my love. There is no curse."

"Then why? What's holding us apart when we are both on this side of life?"

"It's too soon..."

"What do you mean, too soon? I feel as if I've been over here for a whole eternity."

"We can't measure time the same way we do in the physical world, cheri. It is too soon for us to be reunited." Nadine's voice sounded distant as she spoke again. "Paul, there's nothing I'd rather do than be with you, but there's no way I can alter forces that have been set in motion. Don't you understand?"

"No, I don't."

Nadine put her hand on my arm. "Paul, it's too early for you to come over to this side to stay. It isn't meant for you to leave your physical life at this time."

"It's not fair!" I cried.

"We're the ones who are unfair to ourselves. The law of karma is not cruel, only just. Like a pendulum it swings, without anger, without vengeance."

"Then why the punishment?"

"No punishment, dearest. For good or evil, we ourselves set it in motion."

"Then how long will it be before we are reunited?"

She shrugged. "I can't tell, my love. Sooner or later, we shall be together again."

So, it wasn't to be as yet. Another test was there for me to face. Well, I had learned already the futility of rebellion against the unknown laws. Some other score had to be settled.

"What haven't I done yet? What haven't I learned?"

I reached for her but she took a step backward. "Professor Farnsworth will guide you on. Trust him."

I turned as the Professor reentered the room and now he and I were alone again.

"What about my future, Professor?"

"Your future, Jim, is entirely in your own hands. No one can stomp upon your free will. You'll use it as your conscience dictates."

"How soon, Professor?"

"He looked at me intently. "Very soon, Jim."

My heart pounded in my chest. Louise in France. Nadine in Russia. *Russia!* The letter from her husband, Arkady...

"What happened in Russia after I got that letter, Professor?"

Professor Farnsworth sighed. "Before you find out, Jim, there's something else that you have to do first."

*   *   *

Torrents of muddy water, cascading downhill on the side of the pavement, carried twigs that the wind had swept along the way. Through the edge of twilight, varying shades of gray danced and cavorted in the reflection of the dim street lamps, and the wind, the howling wind, sent ripples of water across the highway like the lapping ebb-tide of the sea. Everything wept – the maple trees, the dim shake roofs of clustered communities, the empty sidewalks of San Rafael.

The dark silent streets lay empty of human presence and only an occasional automobile, its tires hissing through the asphalt's wet layer, darted across like a fugitive on the run.

It must have been raining steadily for a long time, for the gutters outside our house were gurgling in a flood of water which I heard rather than saw. In addition to the darkness of the evening, I had difficulty bridging my astral sight to the physical and again, as before, objects appeared shadowy, misty and gray. My inability to see clearly was annoying, especially after the sharply delineated colors of the astral world. I tightened my fists and found that my hands were gripping the steering wheel of my car, thus I knew that the automobile was not visible to the physical world. I pulled up in front of our house, behind Henry Manchester's Mercedes. Although it was discreetly parked by the neighbor's house, I recognized it by the skiing resort stickers on the trunk.

I had no idea of the passage of time. How long has it been since my heart attack? Hours? Days? Was I still clinically dead and were my colleagues still working over me, or was I in a coma being kept alive by life-support machines? All these questions bothered me almost as much as seeing Henry's car at my house. His presence evoked my sharp animosity toward him, even though I realized he was only an incidental link in the chain of my life. It was unfortunate that he was my colleague, a fact which had compounded the problem in the past.

How long ago it all seemed to have happened! In spite of the dark and the rain, my involuntary arrival here had an eerie déjà-vu sequence. I sat in the car and reluctantly watched the flashback of that scene.

*   *   *

That crisp Friday morning, before Steve left for his class in graphic art, he and I talked about his work, and I could see that he was far more interested in art than in medicine. I was upset and wanted to argue with him in favor of a medical career, but as I glanced at my watch, I realized that I was going to be late for my rounds at the hospital, so I dashed off.

While driving down the freeway, I discovered that in my haste to leave the house I had forgotten my briefcase. I had brought home a patient's chart I'd need at the hospital.

I was already twenty minutes away from the house and, cursing my increasing forgetfulness—leaving my stethoscope in odd places in the hospital, forgetting my medical journals at the office—I took the next exit off the freeway, made a U-turn, and sped home.

I screeched to a halt in the driveway of our house, barely missing the fender of the Mercedes parked at the curb. I was in such a hurry, that it wasn't until I reached the back door that I realized the Mercedes in front of our house belonged to my colleague, Henry Manchester. I stood with my hand on the door knob. I was so bewildered by his early visit that I couldn't admit any suspicion to my mind. After all, I had left Gretchen only forty minutes ago, while she was busily scraping grease off a frying pan.

I threw the door open and walked into the kitchen. Henry was sitting at the breakfast table and Gretchen, still dressed in her lacy negligée, was standing over him, one hand on his shoulder, the other pouring coffee into his cup. The newspaper was still lying open on the other side of the table as I had left it after breakfast, and the whole scene could have been incongruously domestic and innocent except for one thing. It was Henry who sat in my chair.

Color suffused Henry's face as he rose from the chair, guilt and embarrassment more eloquent in his eyes than any spoken words.

For a few seconds, no one spoke. It was obvious Henry was at a loss for words and Gretchen stood with the coffee pot still in her hand, her face frozen with shock and surprise.

Finally, Henry found his voice. "Jim, I know this sounds ridiculous, but I was on my way to the golf course and stopped in to say hello. I was leaving now."

"It doesn't look to me as if you were planning to leave." I pointed to his cup of coffee. "Gretchen has just poured you a fresh cup."

Gretchen came alive. "Jim, there's no need to be sarcastic. If you give me a chance, I can explain everything."

I stared at her, too angry to speak.

"Henry was really going to the golf course," Gretchen said, "and on a spur of the moment dropped by, just as he said. The least I could do was offer him a cup of coffee."

"In that negligée?"

Henry moved toward the back door. "Jim, I'll get out. I can hardly blame you for being upset, but for God's sake, believe me I told you the truth, and I'm sorry I stopped by."

He was going to say something else but shook his head and dismissed it with a wave of his hand. That apology, more than anything else he could have said, was an admission of guilt, and yet I was puzzled when I saw a glint of malevolence in his eyes, as if another entity overshadowed him for a second.

When he was gone, I faced Gretchen. Although she stood erect and defiant with her chin up, for a brief moment her defensive mask slipped, exposing raw fear and guilt. Then she regained her composure and eyed me derisively. "Well, you must feel very smug for having caught me by surprise."

"I wasn't trying to catch you in anything. I came back for my briefcase."

Gretchen put down the coffee pot and went to the bedroom. I followed her. Her jeans and T-shirt were thrown on the bed carelessly. She picked them up and started toward the bathroom. Her hands trembled. Her silence was exasperating.

"Gretchen, what the hell are you doing?"

She turned around to face me. "Do you want me to spell it out?"

"You could at least be more...more..." I was choking.

She sniffed. "More apologetic? Why should I? You're so immersed in your medicine that you're totally blind to what goes on around you."

I grabbed her arm but she wrenched herself free. "I've been leading my own life lately, and you're not even aware of it."

I closed my eyes fighting an urge to slap her. With difficulty I whispered, "Why Henry?"

She shrugged. "I went to him the first time when you were at a surgical meeting in Nevada. I was lonely, and I spent the night with him in his apartment." She paused, eyeing me closely. Then she lifted her chin and pursed her lips. "You're never around when I need you and Henry is. He truly loves me!"

"Slut!"

She didn't flinch. "You make me laugh. You've ignored me all our married life, treated me as if I were only a necessary appendage to your programmed, and oh, so dull a life. You have no idea that I am a serious student of metaphysics, that I attend Theosophy meetings in San Francisco, that I read works by Freud and Jung. You see me only as a flighty party girl. I try to cope with our miserable marriage the best I know how, and you stand there insulting me in your righteous indignation. You actually look pompous and funny!"

She put her hand over her mouth and began to laugh, at first in suppressed giggles, then louder and more hysterically.

The shock was not so much in my discovery of her new infidelity, as the knowledge that once again I had become an object of ridicule among my friends, neighbors, and colleagues.

I turned and rushed out of the house.

*   *   *

Henry and I never spoke of that incident again, pretending nothing had ever happened. But now, in my disembodied state, I felt sadness. Outside, the steady rain had not abated. The only sounds around me were the final runoffs from the drainpipes and the low murmur of the water in the gutters. The smell of wetted down dust reached my nostrils through the damp air and suddenly a chill made me shiver. I felt my shoulders and head for wetness but they were dry. I got out of the car in the pouring rain, yet it failed to touch me. I was not subject to the elements of the physical world.

The light went on in our kitchen. Drawn to it like a magnet, I entered the house. My favorite chair in the family room, my desk in the study, familiar objects were all in place. This time, I surveyed them with detached curiosity. A while ago, they belonged to me when I was Jim Braddock and walked this floor with the thud of my physical weight. But now, I was also Etièn Louvois with a beloved wife, Louise, and Count Paul Uvaroff with Nadine, my beloved sister, and the world I belonged to was a wider world, at once more beautiful and yet confusing.

Why had I come back again to Braddock's house at this particular time? Was I still in the emergency room? How long have they been working on me? My God, my cardiac arrest happened in the morning. What time was it there now?

I didn't see Gretchen or Henry, and as I pondered the passing hours, I heard Steve's hurried footsteps. He entered the kitchen, grabbed his papers and ran out to his car. I joined him in the passenger seat by willing myself to be there. He drove recklessly, rounding corners. The streets were beginning to dry and the moon was lighting the dark road. As occasional sob escaped his clenched teeth and I was praying that the tears that rolled down his cheeks would not blind his vision. He drove onto the grounds of his high school, got out of the car and started walking across the empty parking lot.

My peripheral vision was drawn to an empty shack to the left of the lot. On the other side of it, hidden from Steve's view, four teenagers loitered. As Steve approached, they nudged one another with elbows and nasty grins slowly spread on their faces.

I followed Steve across the parking lot. Except for a couple of cars, it was deserted. The asphalt had dried and only a few puddles of water glistened on the ground like shining ink spots. One or two windows were lit in the long brick school building, otherwise it stood brooding and silent like a reluctant bystander about to witness a violent scene.

The meowing of the alley cats emerging from their shelters where they had waited out the storm disturbed the stillness of the evening. They scattered around, brushing their quivering furry bodies against Steve's ankles in hope of a handout. Getting none, they scampered noiselessly away, driven by their feline instinct to a familiar corner. Moments later, a garbage can lid clattered to the ground shattering the tension in the air, and the cats screeched as they fought over their bounty.

Steve's step faltered. Slowing down indecisively, he listened and then abruptly headed toward the noise.

I heaved a sigh of relief. Now, if I could only prevent him from passing the shack where the four thugs waited, I would succeed in averting a confrontation. But how to do it? I was powerless to stop a physical body's movement, or to change its direction.

I watched Steve approach the deadlocked cats, clap his hands, shoo them, and then turn back on his heels. I looked at the school building. The main entrance lay directly in line with where Steve stood and if he went that way, he would bypass the shack. I doubted that the gang would leave their cover and jump him in the open lot in full view of the main entrance.

Who were the four teenagers and what were they doing on the school grounds at night? As my thoughts turned to them, I could see them again and knew instinctively that they were the same foursome whom Steve had caught red-handed vandalizing the school lab. They made no noise and moved with slow deliberation.

I looked them over. The biggest one was a fat bully who issued orders to the others with silent motions. There was a pale redhead with a long giraffe neck and a nervously bobbing Adam's apple who held an object in his shaking hand. Another scrawny kid with tousled hair moved restlessly from one foot to the other and darted furtive glances in the direction of the parking lot. The fourth kid was tall and muscular and completely relaxed as he leaned against the shed drinking beer.

Suddenly, the fat one came alert, raised his hand in a warning gesture and listened.

Steve.

I turned around. The cats were swarming about the garbage can using the upturned lid as a springboard to jump onto the edge. Steve was not there. I heard his steps behind me. He had gone through me without my being aware of it, and had started toward the shack.

I knew that he was going to the library the entrance to which was at the back of the building, where he sometimes liked to do his homework.

I moved to the shack's edge between Steve and the gang. They were poised at the ready to spring at their target. Each one of Steve's steps, muffled by his rubber-soled sneakers reverberated nevertheless in my brain exploding into a drum-like beat, growing louder and more painful as the distance between us narrowed. Steve was now only a couple of yards from the gang but, engrossed in his thoughts, he neither had heard nor paid any attention to the brief click of a switch blade being opened.

A short intake of breath, a clumsy movement, and Steve was alerted. He stopped, listening, and then turned toward the school. But it was too late. Motionless predators moments ago, now the hoodlums moved with rehearsed precision and surrounded Steve, blocking his escape. The sharp thin blade of the knife glittering in each hand, they circled Steve slowly, taunting him with short, jerky thrusts into the air.

All this was done in complete silence. From the expression on Steve's face, I knew that he had recognized them and knew who they were. And knowing, was scared.

My chest heaved with sobs of frustration. I had to stop them. But how? I was unable to thwart the movements of physical bodies, but I couldn't believe that I was unable to do anything at all on the physical plane.

The obvious place to seek help was in the school building where two windows were still lit and someone was inside.

The cats arched their bodies, bared their teeth and hissed at me as I passed them. I lunged at them and they scattered out of my way. They sensed my presence...they *saw* me! Could I attract attention by chasing the cats and making them screech at me? But time was of the essence. Frantic, my heart pounding, I stood on the steps in front of the main entrance searching for a way to create distraction. Slight gusts of wind picked up, scratching the concrete with bits of discarded chewing gum wrappers. A side door near the entrance stood slightly ajar. The wind barely moved it, perhaps a couple of inches, but with the movement came a grinding sharp noise of rusty hinges. I could not move a heavy weight, but an open, swinging door? I had to try. I *had* to make it swing.

In one leap I was at the door grabbing it with both hands. The momentum carried my arms through it without resistance. Without thinking, I tried again with the same result. Lining up my curved hands with the edge of the door as if I were grasping it but not squeezing it, I made one last effort and pushed with all the strength I had. I nearly lost my balance as my body pivoted me around unobstructed.

I stopped, panting. When was I going to learn that no physical contact was possible? I had to try something else. But what? I couldn't touch the door, yet the wind did. The wind! It had managed to move the door without physical arms. That was it. Now more than ever, I had to try again the power of my thought.

I concentrated. At first, nothing happened. The door was swinging ever so slightly in the tiny breeze, not enough to move the rusty hinges. I strained. A stronger gust brushed my face like a cold, ghostly hand. I pictured the wind swinging the door, slamming it with the loudest noise possible and as I thought of it intensely, hysterically, the door began to move slowly, opening wider, faster, grinding the hinges, making them grate and screech louder, rising to a higher and higher pitch until the door hit the wall and boomeranged back, slamming the lock into place.

I could do nothing more. I looked toward the shack praying that I wouldn't see Steve walking toward me in his astral dimension. I saw nothing, but I heard muffled voices and Steve's angry retort. Relieved,

I rushed down the school corridor toward the lighted classroom and pushed myself through the closed door.

*   *   *

Two teachers sat at the desk drinking coffee. School papers lay scattered about them. The younger one of the two, dark-haired and short, lifted his head.

"What was that, Bill?"

The other man, muscular and tall with a short crop of graying hair, looked up. "What do you mean?"

"That noise."

"I didn't hear anything."

"You mean you didn't hear that screeching and grating?"

"Oh, that! Sure I heard it, Ed, but that was just a door slamming shut somewhere."

"Exactly."

"So?"

"Don't you understand?"

"I'm afraid I don't. What are you driving at?"

"That door. Why did it slam?"

"Oh, c'mon, Ed. You haven't been watching all that supernatural stuff on TV lately, have you?"

"Bill, we left the front door unlocked, why would anyone try to open the janitor's door?"

"How do you know it's the janitor's door?"

"Because that's the only one that squeaks like that."

Bill stared at Ed for a moment, and then pushed his chair back. "You made your point. Let's go."

The two men walked down the hall and paused at the front door, peering into the darkness.

"The janitor's door is closed. See for yourself – it's locked."

"Well, write it off to an over-tired imagination."

"Let's go in."

"Wait! I saw something. Over there!"

The younger man pointed in the direction of the shack.

"I can't see that far, Ed. What is it?"

"I thought I saw a few kids scatter. Didn't you hear a scuffle?"

The other man yawned. "Well, they were up to no good, no doubt, and now we scared them away. I'm going inside, it's chilly. Coming in, Ed?'

The younger man moved toward the door indecisively, and then hesitated. Stopping his colleague with his arm, he said quietly, "Bill, let's take a look."

He nodded into the darkness. The two men studied each other for a moment in silence. Then, turning abruptly away from the door, they ran toward the shack.

CHAPTER 12

As I stood wondering, the scene gradually faded, and I found myself facing Professor Farnsworth, this time in his garden, the splendor of peonies and roses all around us.

"Your son is safe, Jim," he said with a smile. "All he has is a superficial cut on his hand and a case of major fright. Good for you in not giving up on your power of thought. You succeeded admirably in what you tried to do."

I heaved a sigh of relief, and then asked, "Come to think of it, why did Steve go to school when I'm still in an emergency room? And another thing, how long have they been working on me? My God, my cardiac arrest happened in the morning and when I followed Steve, it was already dark!"

"They moved you from the ER to the CCU, Jim. Go and see for yourself. It's time for you to go back there. Your wife, incidentally, has been keeping a vigil at the hospital all this time. She and Steve were urged to wait at home but she was so distraught that your colleague, Henry Manchester, drove her home so she could change clothes and then brought her right back. Steve was encouraged to attend to his work and his mind occupied. Now go and work on yourself. And that is an order!"

A hurricane of emotions swept over me. So that's why Henry's car was in our driveway. Relieved, I looked out into the garden. It was so beautiful, so inviting. Why punish myself by leaving this haven to fight for the revival of that dense and damaged body of mine, only to face an uncertain future? I checked myself. Gretchen had been at the hospital for what must be many hours by now. A reckoning time for her as it has been for me over here. After all, there had been our young love and passion in the beginning, a bright future before us, so where had it gone wrong? A flash of warmth spread to my face. Why pretend, why be facetious with myself? I knew perfectly well how the marriage had begun to turn sour, slowly, insidiously, and in the final analysis, nearly tragically.

My pulse skipped a beat. I hadn't died after all, my body was lying down there waiting for me to do something about it. I should will myself into that hospital CCU and knew that I could do it. It wasn't too late. I was being given a chance to remedy the past, to start over with Gretchen, make up to her for having neglected her in this life, to pay, so to speak, a karmic debt for having been cruel to her when she was Irene in Russia.

Russia!

The memory of it kept me sitting in the professor's garden. Louise and Nadine, one and the same soul mate of mine was not in the physical body right now. I yearned to be with her, but it was not to be for some time, for I *sensed* that I had to relive the final chapter of my life in Russia and then return to being Dr.Braddock again.

Russia. That letter from Nadine's husband Arkady, hovered over me as a specter. Something sinister was in that letter, something so frightening that I had not been given the opportunity to read it.

What could have been more wrenching, more painful than losing Nadine?

I closed my eyes and pictured *Otradnoye* in my mind. An intense thought, a concentrated power of will, and there I was, in my beloved family estate where Nadine had died in my arms.

The autumn had begun to do its work. The birch and maple leaves had fallen, covering the garden floor with an ever moving carpet of burnished gold and blood red propelled by the erratic gusts of a whining wind. The intermittent silence sang in a plangent fugue that wrapped me in dread and physical malaise. I stood alone in the garden convulsively clutching the letter in my left hand. I stared down at the crumpled pages.

With trembling fingers that fought me, I started to unfold the two pages but a sudden blast of wind whipped them out of my hands and blew them down the path, toying with them as a cat with a bird. The pages gathered momentum, flew up the lowest step of the gazebo and clung to the next higher one.

Stumbling after them, panting, my stomach tight with sick premonition, I grabbed the pages with both hands, then sat down on the upper step, smoothed out the creases, and started to read.

"I shall come to the point directly," Arkady wrote, *"for you do not deserve the formal salutation of `dear' or `respected'. I intend to be brief, for it is as difficult for me to write this as it no doubt will be for you to read it, albeit for different reasons. I demand that you end your life by whatever means you choose. I am willing to announce your death as accidental, and for that reason it will be easy to say that you were cleaning your shotgun and it discharged in your face. I give you my word of honor as a gentleman, that after your death, the truth of this whole sordid affair will not be revealed to anyone. Should you refuse to follow my order within this week, I shall disclose to the Tsar your incestuous relationship with my wife, thus ruining your career and, unfortunately, Nadine's*

*reputation. Be assured, that my contempt for you is so
great, that I cannot abide the thought of you walking
this earth without retribution, and I shall not hesitate to
follow through on my threats. My sole passion is to see
you dead."*

I staggered into the gazebo and leaned against the railing. I was
choking. The air didn't seem to reach my lungs.

God! To die?...and by my own hand? Damn it, no!

I didn't want to kill myself. A shotgun...To pull the trigger into
my face?...so messy...all that blood... Repugnant.

I dropped the letter and pressed my forehead against the cool
column. The pages rustled, scraped the stone steps and, propelled by
a cowering wind, clung to my boot. I kicked them off, then turned
and paced the gazebo hugging my stomach with both arms to stop
the fluttering inside.

The infamy of Arkady's devious plan...his brutal plot of revenge...
The bastard. The righteous bastard. I pounded my fist against the
marble pillar, the sound of my dry sobs pitiful in the silence.

What irony. When Nadine died, I had wished to join her in that
nebulous world so eloquently described by the church's teachings.
Here was that chance. But to kill myself?

I sat down on a stone bench and with my elbows on my thighs,
held my head between my hands. All of a sudden, life seemed precious.
Could I trust the bastard to honor his promise of calling my death
an accident?

The priests were forbidden to perform funeral services or even to
pray for suicides. The Church taught that it was an act of cowardice,
a sacrilege, a mortal sin. But would my suicide be an act of cowardice?
I, a coward?

What was the alternative? Disgraced, looked upon as a pariah,
my life would be intolerable. But what about Nadine? Beloved Nadine

would be vilified and dishonored. A gentle soul who could not stand up and defend herself against the denunciation of her vengeful, husband.

My suicide would protect her name and honor. So what would the Church say to that? No matter what the cause, the Church would not condone it. But that was all rhetoric, wasn't it? The Church would never learn the true cause of my death if Arkady carried out his promise. After all, it should be in his own interests not to dishonor his wife's name.

I wanted to kill him. To strangle him slowly with my hands and watch him die.

In a few moments, the passion of hate gave in to logic. A murder investigation would create a different kind of scandal, and grudgingly, I had to believe that Arkady would not divulge the truth. There was no other way but to carry out his order.

I looked around me. I was sitting not far from the spot where Nadine had died. Here is where I held her against my chest, her hair fragrant with the extract of roses. I had often hugged and kissed her as a brother, but oh, how often I had longed to touch her the other way. Forbidden way of Eros. All at once, I felt a stirring in my groin. What price unrequited love! I took a deep breath and looked at the garden.

The wind had subsided and the rolling leaves rested at my feet. The luxurious fluffy tail of a shy squirrel flipped between the stone gazebo railings. Its whiskers twitching, the curious creature looked me over, then raced up the nearest tree. A sparrow, perched on a thin branch of an elm, chirped happily, cocked its head and flew away. A wave of calm washed over me filling me with determination.

Our parents left *Otradnoye* to Nadine, and now our family estate belonged to me. But the soul of the place was gone. I rose and as I took a step down from the gazebo, I saw that Arkady's letter was still lying on the ground. I quickly picked it up. No one must see it. I walked slowly to the house without looking back at the gazebo. Arkady had moved to St. Petersburg and I had been planning to leave as well. Once inside, I passed through the parlor, its furniture now covered with white sheets, as the servants were preparing to close up the house for the winter. Their distant murmur wafted from the kitchen along with the smell of simmering borscht and baking kasha. Let the living enjoy their food. I no longer belonged to this world. I yearned to join Nadine who was waiting for me just beyond the veil of physical life.

Exhilaration propelled me toward my study where my cabinet stood filled with a collection of shotguns, pistols, and rifles. I opened the glass door and studied the weapons for a few minutes. They were carefully lined up in the gun rack and had not been disturbed for many years. I pulled out the shotgun with a carved and silver-trimmed handle that belonged to my father. Then I reached down to the floor of the cabinet and took out the necessary tools to clean the shotgun and to load it. It gave me a sensual pleasure to caress its polished wood and a perverse satisfaction that such a beautiful piece of workmanship would be the instrument of my imminent death.

A sudden thought struck me. What if Arkady should change his mind later on and betray the secret of my death? A cold shiver ran through me as my hand clutched convulsively the barrel of the gun. I leaned it against my chair, rose, and walked over to the fireplace where the wood was crackling in the fire. I pulled Arkady's letter out of my pocket and threw it in. With burning hatred I watched it scorch and turn to ashes. Slowly I turned and went to my desk. Dipping my quill in the ink well, I wrote on my note pad: "Things to do today, 15 October, 1881: Answer letters. Check that my uniform is ready to wear. Clean the pistol, rifle, and shotgun. Things to do tomorrow, October 16, 1881: Close the house. Leave for the city." I blotted the ink and felt smug about this. Arkady could not destroy the note for he was already in the city and when the servants find me, they will turn over the note to the police. No one would doubt that my death was accidental after reading the plans I made for the two days.

Next, I took out of the cabinet my father's pistol and cleaned it, together with the rifle. To make it more believable, I did not replace them into the cabinet, but lay them down on the leather sofa that stood against the wall, thus setting up an unfinished scene with the cabinet door open.

I ran my hand along my chin and felt the afternoon stubble on my jawbone. I hurried to my bed chamber where in the alcove next to it I picked up my razor, sharpened it on the leather strop, lathered my face and started to shave. Half way through, I started to laugh, the sound of it reverberating with a hollow echo in my ears. What was I thinking? The shotgun aimed at my face will take care of any unseemly stubble I may have developed since that morning. Carefully, I cleaned my face and replaced the razor where I had found it, so that the servants wouldn't wonder why I decided to shave a second time during the day.

Back in my chair, I picked up the shotgun, loaded it and placed it between my legs. For the last time I looked around my study, an elegant room furnished in Karelian warm woods and seasoned leather chairs. Beside the gun cabinet, the wall was lined with shelves filled to capacity with books. My loving glance skimmed the authors' names. Pushkin, Tolstoy, Turgenev, Voltaire, Victor Hugo, Dumas, Shakespeare, all read and reread, except the latest novel by Dostoyevsky, the Brothers Karamazov, published last year. I had spent so much of my time tending to and worrying about Nadine that I could not concentrate on reading that new work.

I set the shotgun aside, went over to the bookshelf, picked up the volume, leafed through it. The words trembled before my eyes and none reached my mind. I replaced the book and turned away.

On the other side of the room, near my desk, stood a sideboard with a silver tray and crystal glasses on it. My eye was caught by a decanter of brandy and I was instantly drawn to it. Why not? It may ease the pain. I poured myself a full glass of the amber colored liquid and walked to the window.

The wind had slipped away and the weeping willow by the pond stood pensive and detached from human turmoil. The garden, bereft of human presence, no longer beckoned me into its fold. It was no longer mine. Nadine, our parents, and soon I will have left it to the living. *Otradnoye* was now Arkady's. My pulse quickened, flushing my temples with a throbbing pain. What will my murderer do with it? Sell it to another family who will never know the monstrous treachery perpetrated by the former owner within its walls?

It started to rain, gently at first, then recklessly in tune with the tears that poured down my face and ultimately washed my soul of fear. I downed the brandy in a few gulps and was about to dash the glass against the fireplace when a sobering thought stayed my hand. I was not alone in the house. The sound of broken glass would bring the servants into the room. I replaced the glass on the tray and holding onto my courage, hurried to the chair where I left the shotgun.

With my face over it now, I whispered, "Nadine, the love of my life."

Then I leaned over the barrel of the gun, put it in my mouth and pulled the trigger.

CHAPTER 13

I came to, shivering, and found myself sitting across from Professor Farnsworth in his garden.

"What happened to me after my suicide, Professor?" I asked. "Was I reunited with Nadine? Did I suffer the tortures of hell, as the church warns, for ending my life?"

Professor Farnsworth patted me on the back. "Not at all. Don't forget that you didn't *want* to die. Yours was a sacrifice to protect your sister's good name. It's quite different for the one who kills himself to escape from his troubles. Without his physical body, his emotions are intensified. *That* is the true hell."

"And how long does his hell last?"

"For as long as his physical span of life would have lasted. If only the suicides knew they would suffer more on this side, they would think twice before taking their lives. But to answer your other question, yes, you were reunited with Nadine. You haven't lost her."

Professor Farnsworth smiled and rose. "And now, Jim, I must say goodbye. It is time for you to return to Gretchen."

The professor's last words faded and I was alone. Although I found much beauty in this discarnate existence, still, after reliving the traumatic last chapter of my Russian life, I knew there was unfinished business I had to take care of in my physical body.

The urge to wake up in CCU where I was being worked on, seized me. I was ready to let go of my Russian incarnation and only one question remained unanswered. Where was Arkady now, the man who sent me to my death? A twinge of fear nibbled at my nerves. Is he someone I know in my present life as Braddock? And who was he in the French incarnation? Was he the court physician Fagon whom I had despised and whom I hated through the long years as a monk?

Yes, that seemed logical. As Fagon in France he had caused my beloved Louise's death, and as Arkady, he had caused mine.

So my encounter with him in Russia was not the last one. He would surely surface somewhere in this incarnation or the next.

I sighed, distancing myself from the professor's peaceful garden. I was ready, no, eager for the challenge that awaited me.

*   *   *

I heard voices, distant and muffled. Not fully conscious, blissfully ignorant of recent past, I was aware of being in limbo, suspended in time. Slowly I opened my eyes and was momentarily blinded by strong lights. I stood by the side of the bed in the CCU on which my body was lying. My two colleagues, Bob Rice, and Sam Weaver, together with three nurses, were bent over me firing questions and answers at one another.

"All right! He's in sinus!"

"Did we get any blood pressure?"

"Yes, doctor. 120 over 80."

"Perfect!"

I could hear them heave a deep sigh of relief, then Sam Weaver said, "We've finally got him with good rhythm and BP at last. Let's go ahead, hook him up to the ventilator with FIO 2 of 50% and we'll check some gases in about half an hour. We'll leave him on lidocaine drip at 2 mg and watch him through the night."

I stood there smiling and shaking my head in admiration. They did exactly as I would have in the same situation. Now everyone was quiet, worried that I might crash again. I could see one nurse sitting back in obvious relief that everything was stable and most certainly annoyed that now she had to clean up the mess: the drug boxes, the wraps, the pads, syringes, packs all over the place.

As peace descended in the CCU, I felt a strong pull toward my body. As I came in contact with it, I blacked out.

*   *   *

Sounds. A humming and swooshing sound, a rhythmic blip above my head. All those machines designed to sustain life. All those tubes that must be running in and out of my body. I didn't want to see them. There was something inhuman, degrading in being placed on automatic pilot. I'd seen enough watching my patients dehumanized, dependent on these inanimate wonders of modern science. Yes, I'd watched enough in totally detached manner, concerned only with the results of my surgical procedures, until I myself had become the patient.

Now I heard voices. A man's. A woman's. Whispers really, floating somewhere above me on the periphery of my consciousness. Soft and distant at first, fading in and out, they grew louder, then lost their soothing rhythm and became words.

"How long, doctor? How long yet before he regains consciousness?"

Gretchen. A trembling voice, teary and frightened.

"I don't know, Mrs. Braddock. I don't like to even venture a guess. We can only hope it will be soon. Your husband had a coronary occlusion and he is one of the cases we won. Twenty to twenty-five percent of people who have coronary occlusion will drop dead, and of the rest half will be revived and half will linger for a while. Each case is different. Your husband was one of the lucky ones."

Mrs. Braddock... Each case... Must be a young intern not to be calling Gretchen by her first name. Someone who is thinking of me as a 'case' not as Dr. Braddock. Patients are people, not 'cases' - call me by my name! How painful to hear this on the receiving end especially when I had been guilty of the same fault.

"You shouldn't be sitting here, Mrs. Braddock," the doctor was saying. "You've been here for many hours. You need to rest. We'll call you immediately if any signs of awareness appear in your husband."

I hear a scraping of the chair by my bed. "I can't rest, doctor. I'll be out in the lounge. At the first sign of *anything*, do you hear? I want to be called."

I didn't want her to leave. But raising my voice to call her back was too much of a struggle. What was I thinking? There was an endotracheal tube in my throat. I couldn't speak even if I were strong enough to do so. With an enormous exercise of will power, I concentrated on moving the fingers of my right hand. I managed. Slightly. Gretchen, who was evidently still in the room, cried out my name and was back at my side, kissing my hand and weeping. "He's coming out of it, Doctor! Here, did you see? His fingers moved!"

"Mrs. Braddock, please, move away. Here, let me help you up."

She must have been kneeling beside my bed. I felt the warm, moist touch of her lips as she raised my hand to her face. The feeling was wonderful. It surprised me. This simple physical contact made me want desperately to see her, and to hell with all the tubes and machines that were around me.

My eyelids fluttered, I felt dizzy, but I struggled and finally opened my eyes. Gretchen's face swam above me, her tears dropping on my face, her smile so loving, so relieved that I tried to say "I love you", forgetting that I couldn't because of the blasted tube in my throat.

"Mrs.Braddock, please, I must insist that you leave the room!"

Reluctantly, Gretchen rose and stepped back. The attending physician bent over me. "Dr.Braddock, please blink your eyes if you understand me."

I blinked. That small effort seemed enormous and I slipped back into unconsciousness. When I opened my eyes again, Gretchen was stroking my arm gently and smiling.

"Darling," she said softly, "the doctor says you're going to be O.K."

She moved closer and rubbed her cheek on my arm. "I dare not touch you more, all those needles and tubes...I'm afraid to dislodge them. The doctor said...oh God, darling, you gave us such a scare! Steve will be here soon. We're so relieved!"

I couldn't move my head toward her. The tube was in the way and besides, it seemed too much of an effort. I looked at her and wiggled my fingers. She slid her hand down and squeezed them gently.

"The doctor said that if you continue improving, he'll take the tube out and then you'll be able to talk."

I was glad I had survived. The image of Professor Farnsworth faded, but the memory of what I relived and learned while out of body remained vivid.

I heard a slight commotion, whispers, movement near my bed and when I opened my eyes again, Bob Rice and Sam Weaver were smiling at me. "You went into sudden cardiac arrest, friend," Sam said. "You have a moderate amount of heart damage but as you can see, you survived."

Bob Rice shook his finger at me. "You scared the hell out of us. It took us a long time to win this one. We'll get you for this!"

I tried to smile, but failed.

Another commotion, more whispers and there was Steve touching my shoulder with a gentle hand.

"Hi, Dad! Sure gave us a fit. You look awesome. Glad you're back with us. Hey, you take it easy now, O.K.?"

Awkward, frightened, but my dear beloved son. And Gretchen. They were my priority, not this blasted hospital. God willing, everything will take its proper place in my life from now on. I tried to sigh but short jerky gasps came out instead. With my eyes closed, I moved the fingers of both hands this time and tried to smile.

"Try to sleep, my love," I heard Gretchen whisper.

*   *   *

Recovery was slow but uneventful. The endotracheal tube was removed for good about an hour after I finally regained consciousness. Within a few days, I was transferred to a cardiology ward and was encouraged to get out of bed and walk. A week later, Gretchen took me home.

God, it was good to see our home again, to enter our sunny family room and sit in my favorite recliner. Gretchen fussed, wanted me to go to bed immediately, but I knew that the best thing for me was to be up and around for as long my stamina allowed. I wanted to regain strength as fast as I could, to be in control of my body again, but most of all, to be a husband and father first and physician and surgeon second.

As days progressed, I could see a wondrous change taking place in Gretchen. I had forgotten how affectionate she could be. A pink glow appeared on her cheeks, and a sweet, dreamy smile played on her lips. All of a sudden memories of our early years together came flooding back.

Gretchen had always been full of life and joy. She loved people. In the past, not a week went by that she wouldn't ask me, "Honey, why don't we invite someone over for a drink?" or, "We have a free week coming up, why don't we ask a few of your residents for a buffet dinner?" Never was there a cake on the table that she wouldn't share a portion of it with a lonely neighbor. She had so much love to give.

As I thought back on the passage of time, I realized that she had gradually lost that *joie de vivre* I loved in her so much in the beginning. How could I have failed to look within myself and ask if possibly I had something to do with the widening distance between us and the anger that corroded our love? How grateful I was now for having come to my senses before it was too late. I'd learned a lot while in my out of body existence. I was now a changed man, ready to make up for lost time.

*   *   *

The days were getting shorter, so I tried to get home as early as I could, to sit outside on our roofed patio and enjoy our pre-dinner drinks, as usual, martini for me and a bourbon and coke for her. Coming home early was an unheard of situation in the past, for I always lingered in the office to finish my paper work, subconsciously delaying going home. But now, I hurried home with thrilling anticipation.

One afternoon, about a month after my hospital stint, we were sitting in our comfortable wicker chairs on the patio. As we watched the sunset, I reached for her hand and kissed it gently. She pulled it away abruptly and walked back into the house. I was crestfallen that my tentative overture was rejected.

I looked beyond our small garden. The approaching dusk muted the magenta sunset, wrapped the grass and oak trees in a haze. The darkening landscape had darkened my mind as well. I had never been articulate in expressing my innermost feelings and now I brooded over my inability to convey to Gretchen that I had changed, that I had learned a wrenching lesson and was trying to make amends. More than that, I longed to reestablish our lovemaking not as a duty, but with the renewed ardor of years long past.

Deep in my introspection, I did not hear her footsteps behind me until she threw a mohair comforter over my legs, tucked it in under my thighs, and with a smile resumed her seat beside me. After a while, the ice cubes in my martini melted and I rose to replenish my glass. As I turned toward the patio door, I noticed that Gretchen was hugging herself and that her bare upper arms were covered with gooseflesh. It suddenly occurred to me that it was always she who had watched over my health, consistently bringing me a sweater or a blanket throw and I had always taken it for granted that she would take care of herself as well.

Those were the little gestures of affection, the little pleasures of life that showed thoughtful concern for each other's comfort. And I had failed miserably in the past.

I went to the kitchen, refilled my glass with ice cubes and the remaining martini from the silver shaker, picked up my glass and stopped. There I was again, failing to check if Gretchen needed a refill as well. I placed my glass back on the kitchen counter, went to the bedroom closet, pulled one of her sweaters off the hanger and returning to the patio, gently wrapped it around her shoulders. She started, then raised her surprised face to me. "Thank you," she whispered. I picked up her glass and raised my brows in a silent question. She laughed and nodded. "Might as well have another one."

Back by her side with our drinks on the small glass table in front of us, I turned toward her. "Gretchen, I want to...I mean..." I cleared my throat, "we need to talk."

Her face clouded. "Back to the old habits, right? What have I done now? Please don't start preaching again."

"I deserve that. Please listen and I'll explain."

"So what is it you want to tell me this time?" After setting her drink on the coffee table, Gretchen folded her hands on her lap and sat up stiffly.

I studied her for a few moments, searching for the right words. At forty-five, she was still lovely. Her creamy complexion was remarkably smooth and her green eyes hadn't lost their luster. Only her red hair had darkened over the years but there was no trace of gray as yet. Her lips were pressed tensely in anticipation of what undoubtedly, she thought was going to be an unpleasant dialogue.

I sighed. "Darling, I vowed never to preach to you again. A tall order, to be sure, but I'm going to try my damnest to change, be a better husband. I'll probably fail a few times – old habits die hard -- but I'm going to try."

"And just how are you going to accomplish that? Are you telling me that you're really going to change after a twenty-year habit? I don't believe you."

She sounded bitter and I couldn't blame her.

"Please, darling, listen to me first. I've been selfish and egotistical and I need to clear the air, get things off my chest. I simply took it for granted that I was a good husband providing you with comfort and security. I guess I looked at you more as--as--"

"an appendage to your life." Gretchen supplied the words bitterly.

"No. Just less than an equal partner in our marriage. I never stopped to think that it takes two people to make a marriage work and simply assumed that you would be happy with me the way things were."

Gretchen leaned forward, shock and surprise written all over her face. "Why this confession, this self-deprecation? It's so out of character for you, you—you the macho surgeon, the self-assured husband, so intolerant of any encroachment on your own chosen time. What happened, Jim, that made you want to change? I must know."

The last words were spoken gently, almost pleadingly.

But I could not tell her of my out of body experiences, although I knew that she would believe me. Yet there was real danger in telling her about it. How could I tell her of my encounter with her as Irene in Russia, my guilt about it, and the desire to wipe the slate clean? She knew too much of reincarnation theory not to suspect that once again my motives were egotistical, that I was trying to make up to her for my own selfish reasons rather than for her happiness. I could never convince her that I had realized how good and loyal a person she had been as Irene in Russia, how unselfish her motives then, and that I had come to see her now as a singularly warm and caring person in this life as well. It wasn't just my desire to wipe out a debt, but a genuine, growing love that was deepening with every passing hour. Her beauty and sex appeal were always there, but it was only now that I responded to them with full force, stronger than I had ever felt for her before. A force that sent a delicious tremor through my body.

Although Gretchen believed in reincarnation, I was still reluctant to tell her about my experiences on the *other side of life*. So, I latched onto a half-truth. "Darling, I am neither the first nor the last person whose near-death experience has turned me around and made me take stock of my life. You've heard of sudden revelations where your whole life flashes before you and spontaneously you see it from a different perspective."

Gretchen nodded slowly but I could see that she was not entirely convinced.

Hesitantly, I took her hand. "Darling, let's pretend the past was a bad dream. A hard learning experience."

"Only time will tell if you've really changed." She chewed on her lips for a few seconds, then suddenly her eyes filled with tears. "Jim, it's not all one-sided. I was wrong as well. We should have gone to a counselor, discussed our problems and maybe a lot could have been avoided. But I was convinced that you wouldn't agree to do that, that your ego and pride would not allow you to even admit that there was anything wrong with our relationship. At that time, you would have blamed it all on me."

I winced at her words because she was right and it was not easy to hear. She saw my reaction. "Please, hear me out. I know it's not pleasant, but believe me, I'm not throwing accusations at you for the past, but only trying in my own way to explain, if not justify my...my... fling with Tom and later with Henry, and--and that other incident..." She flushed with embarrassment and I knew what she was trying to say, but I remained silent and let her go on.

"I was angry, frustrated by lack of attention from you, for not seeing me as a person with my own needs. I felt that you never really *saw* me as a separate human being, so I turned to the first man who paid attention to me, admired me, pursued me. Can you at least understand that, if not forgive?" She looked at me with pleading eyes and I nodded a couple of times, still finding it hard to speak.

"I never singled out those two men. Believe me when I say that they came on to me. I was starved for attention and affection, and...I have to admit, I was flattered. And then, when it happened, I wanted you to find out, to hurt you, to make you jealous, to make you come back to me. I realize now what folly that was, and it's a miracle that it didn't break up our marriage."

I shook my head. "Darling, please..." She put her hand over my mouth.

"Don't! Don't say it! Your gestures, the things you've done just now are much more important to me than any words." Suddenly she folded upon herself and burst out crying, covering her face with her hands. "Jim, darling, I want you to know... there was no one...I mean no one I ever loved but you...I have to say..."

I pulled her hands away from her face. "We love each other and that's all we must remember. Why dig up the past? The present is what matters. I've been a bastard, and I'll try hard to make up to you." I paused and smoothed her hair. "But darling, be patient with me. It may not always go smoothly, but I'll do my darnest not to be a pompous ass!"

She lifted her head to me, a look of surprise and love all over her tear-stained face. Then she started laughing. "I'm sorry Jim, but it is all so sudden. I couldn't ever imagine you calling yourself a pompous ass!"

I realized how incongruous my outburst must have sounded to her and started to laugh as well. I lifted her out of her chair and set her down on my lap. She squirmed and looked over her shoulder. "What if Steve comes out with one of his endless biology questions?"

"Sooo...?" I grinned, delighted by her reaction.

"What do you mean, `soo', you know darn well what I mean. He'll think we've gone bonkers, two old parents necking."

"Not so old," I countered. "Nothing old in being middle-aged. Besides," I looked her up and down with what I hoped was a lecherous look, "you're sexier now than ever before."

True enough, Steve did show up at the door, not to ask a chemistry question, but to say that he was going to a movie with a girlfriend. This being Friday night, we didn't object. In a few minutes his car roared out of the garage and he was gone.

"So much for homework," I said laughing.

Gretchen echoed me with her own bell-like laugh. "I suppose we must give him some latitude. After all, he'll be off to college next year."

I leaned over her. "Oh, Gretchen, darling," I whispered and kissed her hard on the mouth.

To my shock, she responded with the kind of passion I hadn't experienced since the early years of our marriage. My head spun. I wanted her and trembled from fear of rejection, but Gretchen's hands were all over me, frantic, searching, clawing at my jacket and shirt.

Blood pulsated through my veins, my body throbbing, demanding release. Without a word, I rose, took her hand and pulled her toward our bedroom. My sexy wife turned on all the lights. I reached for her again, and we tore at each other's clothes, dropping them on the floor as we inched our way to the bed.

It was wonderful. I had forgotten how thrilling it could be to let our bodies join in one long thrust of passion with no reservations. Gretchen responded with equal abandon, starved for my loving. I reveled in her still youthful body.

What a fool I had been to have neglected her all these years, using sex as a mechanical release without a thought of mutual satisfaction, the very spark that ignited response in both of us. And she, that kittenish wife of mine did not leave me wondering if she had been satisfied. The aftermath of our lovemaking was as sweet as the act itself. We lay in each other's arms, entwining our bodies into a fusion of tenderness, clinging to each other as if our lives depended on it. I threw the blanket off and stroked her silken skin, gently rediscovering the mounds and valleys of her torso, showering feathery kisses on her face and neck.

She reached up to kiss me back. "Oh, Jim," her whisper tickled my neck where she had buried her face.

I smothered her words with a deep and tender kiss. I didn't want to hear anything. Our kind of silence was replete with understanding, a comforting silence that said all, forgave all, and wrapped us in the magic of a new beginning.

*   *   *

I returned to work full time but made my own decision. I no longer sought excuses to work overtime. I took my turn being on call weekends, but used my heart attack as a reason for not taking extra calls or substituting for another surgeon. The only exceptions were emergencies when the attending physician was out of town.

How happy I was for having been given this opportunity to wipe out my debt to Gretchen-Irene in this life and I wondered how much more of a debt I would have accumulated if I hadn't had that brush with death. From time to time my mother's homey asides would come to mind and one in particular stuck in my memory, "Something good always comes out of a bad situation," she would say nodding.

I spent weekends with Gretchen and Steve, both of whom responded to me with ill-concealed delight. Late afternoon was my favorite time of the day. We all gathered in that cozy room to watch the evening news—Gretchen and I with our drinks, Steve with a Pepsi. Then Gretchen would go into the kitchen to get the dinner ready while Steve and I talked softly about the events of the day, whether political or social, or his current studies at school. I was vastly pleased to see in him a keen mind and an acute sense of deductive logic and told him so.

One afternoon as we were sitting in the family room by the lighted fire, waiting for Gretchen to call us to dinner, Steve put down his sports magazine, rose from his chair and started to pace the floor in front of me, rubbing his hands and avoiding my gaze. Then he stopped abruptly, took a deep breath and blurted out, "Dad, I need to talk to you about something."

"Sure," I said, putting down my magazine and looking at him over my glasses. He was a good-looking kid with the red hair and green eyes he inherited from his mother and a firm jaw line that was mine.

Steve looked at me briefly and then looked at his hands. "Dad, I don't want to go to medical school."

"I suspected as much, son. I watched your attitude during your science projects, and your reactions to your graphic art assignments.

I guess I fooled myself into believing that the stress I was noticing in your science work was just your desire to do your best."

Steve looked at me stunned. "Then you're not mad at me?"

"No. I wouldn't be honest if I said I'm not disappointed, but at least I'm not surprised." I paused for a moment, weighing my words. Down deep I knew that a medical career would be a burden for Steve, that right from the beginning he tried to please me, aware of how much I wanted him to follow in my footsteps. I had been deluding myself all along, and yet I realized that had he told me this before my heart attack, the uncompromising egotist in me would have been incensed and used all tactics of intimidation to make him stick with medicine. I suppressed a smile. *What do you know,* I thought, *I've come a long way from the arrogant, self-serving surgeon to a humble human being!*

"There is nothing worse, Steve, than spending your life in a profession that was forced upon you. Above all, I want to see you happy in whatever career you choose. I'm glad you made your decision now rather than half-way through medical school."

"Dad, why wasn't I influenced by your enthusiasm in medicine? I agonized over it for such a long time."

I shrugged. "Damn if I know the answer. All the trite platitudes one hears in favor of medicine don't hold any water. Whatever urge you have in your gut, you have to follow it. In fact, I'm rather proud that you found the courage to tell me about it now, especially when you expected me to get mad."

Steve grinned but continued to sneak a searching glance at my face, no doubt having a hard time believing my easy reaction.

"You know what I like about you, Dad?" Steve said finally with an admiring grin, "You're so understanding. I never knew you had it in you until we started talking about things recently." He paused, then asked, "Are you sure you are not mad at me?"

I chuckled. "Do I look mad? No, Steve. I told you I'm disappointed but not surprised and certainly not angry. Now what do you say we go and see what your mother is doing in the kitchen before we both get maudlin?"

Steve laughed and we rose to join Gretchen.

CHAPTER 14

Life seemed to go on smoothly and my happiness should have been complete, but no, I began to be plagued by harrowing dreams, vivid and persistent and disturbing. As if my experiences while on the verge of death were not enough, they came back to haunt me, and I could not decipher the reasons for their return. What was it that needed to be done, what was it that I could not interpret correctly, what was it that was left unfinished, and how was I to learn it?

I realized that this time it was up to me alone to understand what was yet to be done without the professor's help. He had once said that to instruct me in what to do was an infringement on my will. Our own decision to do right is the one most important thing for the soul's redemption, he had said.

And so I struggled, knowing instinctively that the dreams were warning me that the final test was about to happen and I was being prepared to face it.

The dreams were repetitive and with minor variations underscored my loathing for Fagon in France and my hatred for Arkady in Russia. Little by little, I became convinced that Fagon and Arkady were one and the same soul and that far from having worked out that emotional tie, there still remained an unresolved issue between us.

In France, my dreams were confined to Louise and the Sun King's final hours when Fagon in his pompous arrogance was rude to his subordinates, and virtually ignored my presence. Bitterness and anger against him were mine again as I watched in silence the slow approach of the Sun King's death.

But these suppressed emotions I suffered at Fagon's hands were nothing compared to the violent, burgeoning hatred I nourished in my heart for Arkady when in my dreams I relived the same scenario of his insults and demands for my death.

And then came the latest dream in Russia. Again the park in *Otradnoye*, again the gazebo, again Arkady with that air of superiority on his aging face, and a nervous twitch in one eyelid as he watches me hold his letter in my trembling hand.

"The likes of you," he is saying with venom in his voice, "should be chained and paraded down the streets as perverts who broke the law of nature set down by God."

I make an effort to say something, but he raises his hand imperiously. "You revolt me, do you hear?" His voice is rising. "You have no alternative but to die, so the ground you walk on will no longer be polluted by your presence."

He looks at me in triumph, this self-righteous, virulent man, and I can no longer contain myself.

I rush at him, grab him by the throat and squeeze it, relishing the sight of his bulging eyes, the sudden terror in his face, the instant reversal of the power one held over the other. As soon as I drop him, he rises, brushes his coat and with a superior smile says, "Don't you know that you can't kill me in this life? I'm still alive!"

*   *   *

"Jim, Jim, wake up!"

I heard Gretchen's voice and felt her hand shake my shoulder. I sat up in bed, heart pounding, and checked the clock. 2 a.m.

"You were moaning, thrashing in bed. A nightmare?" she asked solicitously. I nodded, not daring to speak and rolled over to my side, pretending to go back to sleep. But sleep didn't come. Unnerved by the dream, I was well aware that in my Russian life I did kill myself, but my subconscious desire for vengeance would not let me rest.

For a week or so after that dream, I was constantly on the alert for something to happen. But what awaited me? What form of retribution would face me, and in spite of all that I had endured, would I have the moral strength to do the right thing? The waiting and my runaway imagination were akin to torture. Every day I looked at every man on the floor of the hospital. I searched their faces dreading to recognize any fleeting resemblance to the Arkady of my dreams.

Before long, Gretchen noticed my nervousness. "Is anything wrong, Jim? Something at the hospital?"

I shook my head and tried to smile. "No, dear, just extra work piling up. It does happen periodically."

She looked at me in silence and I knew she did not believe me. "Did I do something wrong?" Her voice was small and pitiful. Shamed, I took her in my arms and held her close. "Of course not, my darling. I had a few days of stress, that's all. I'll be O.K. Please bear with me."

She snuggled close to my chest. "You shouldn't have this much stress after your heart attack. Please cut down your patient load!" She raised her head with such pleading in her face that I kissed her on the mouth deeply. For the next hour I forgot all about my fears and made Gretchen forget her concerns about me.

Yet as the days went on, I fretted and waited.

*   *   *

Weeks went by and spring was in full bloom. Driving daily across the Golden Gate Bridge I never ceased to marvel how beautiful the San Francisco skyline was with its cluster of skyscrapers rising majestically above low stretches of milky fog. Below the bridge, the boisterous waters of the Bay were frequently studded with windblown sails of small boats. Going home from the city however, especially after a busy day at the hospital, I thrilled at the splendor of Marin County - hills and valleys rich with thick foliage and trees of flowering crepe myrtle and crabapple in delicate pinks and whites.

I settled into a slower routine of seeing patients in my office and doing daily rounds at the hospital. The frantic pressure of former years was a thing of the past and I wondered why I hadn't done this long before now. The answer was obvious. It would have never occurred to me that I was ruining my life and health by driving myself beyond the normal limits of a busy practice. How sad that it took a near tragedy to make me place things in proper perspective, to stand back and see my life objectively.

Economically, my practice didn't suffer and there was plenty of money for a comfortable life, a handsome savings account for Steve's college and even a luxurious trip abroad we began to plan. Gretchen wanted to visit her home town in Germany and I was eager to relive those days of courtship. After that we planned to drive south to Bavaria and Austria.

So life had become rewarding and I felt as if Gretchen and I were enjoying another honeymoon, this time more meaningful after the trauma of the past few years. I was given a second chance at life not only because of the expert medical team of my colleagues who had saved me, but also because of the revelations I had that showed me what life was all about and how I had wronged Gretchen.

I knew that I had to work out my relationship with Gretchen before I could be with Nadine again. As it was, I was learning to appreciate Gretchen more and more and understood that her affairs had been a cry for help – desperate moves to attract my attention.

*   *   *

A few weeks before we were to embark on our European trip, I was strolling down the hospital corridor after having just finished rounds when the loudspeaker blared, "Code Blue! Code Blue!" Dr.Braddock to the ER! Dr.Braddock to the ER, please."

I was on call that day, so I ran to the emergency room and faced pandemonium. Several gurneys stood along the wall with bloodied men and women brought in from the city streets probably after a gang-related fight or car accidents. None seemed in a life-or-death situation, so I rushed to the far end of the room where the nurses and the attending intern were bending over a body on a gurney.

As I approached, Betty Larson, the emergency room nurse who had helped me on many occasions, raised her head and waved to me.

I hurried over and bent over the gurney to look at the man's face. He moaned and opened his unfocused eyes.

For an instant, Arkady's face stared back at me. With a sharp intake of breath I blinked, trying to clear my suddenly blurred vision. I stooped lower to take a closer look. When his eyes closed again, I recognized Henry Manchester.

"Dr.Braddock, we have a multiple trauma victim here with internal injuries," the nurse said. "The medics reported that Dr. Manchester was crossing the street when he was hit by a minivan and thrown 20 feet. He was unconscious with a weak pulse. They intubated at the scene and his neuro checks appear stable. He also seems to have injuries to the abdomen with girth dimensions increasing and possible lower extremity fractures."

After giving me this terse report, she stepped aside, allowing me to take a better assessment. Indeed, his girth was firm and expanding, indicating active internal bleeding. For a few moments I stood frozen on the spot. How I had hoped that my final confrontation with Arkady would be postponed until some other life! My heart pounded in my chest painfully. The man's life was in my hands. How easy it would be now to hesitate and botch the job to settle the score with the man who had so wronged me. A life for a life.

I knew better. Betraying my Hippocratic Oath was bad enough, but there were other issues at stake.

"Dr.Braddock?"

The nurse brought me up short. *What in the hell am I thinking?* I began barking out orders. "Betty, prep him for surgery and type and cross for four units of whole blood. Who is the ortho on call?"

After I made the incision, I blindly waded through the sea of red to locate a ruptured spleen and quickly tied off the culprit vessel. Then I painstakingly worked to remove the damaged organ and surrounding torn fragments. Surgery was challenging due to the copious amount of blood loss. The X-ray reports revealed three fractured ribs, a fracture of the right hip and a compound fractureof the right femur. My part was done, now the orthopedic surgeon would take another three hours to stabilize the fractures, making for a tedious, long night.

Wearily I situated myself on one of the well-worn sofas in the doctor's lounge. Then I called Gretchen, told her what had happened and that I would be staying the night at the hospital.

She gasped when I mentioned Henry's name and then listened without interrupting until I finished giving her the details.

"What are his chances, Jim?" she asked in a barely audible voice.

I wouldn't commit myself. "He's young and strong, and we're doing all we can to save him."

Arkady not only wronged me in Russia, but as Henry Manchester, he had wronged me again, yet I didn't want him to die. I knew that revenge would never break the vicious circle between us. I was shown my past lives, I was given a glimpse into the good and the bad of them, had attempted to right the wrong, but in the process could not burn out the desire for my past love, or the yearning for another opportunity for happiness.

Well, the laws of nature are immutable and wishful thinking was a waste of time. At that moment saving Henry's life was paramount in my mind. Exhausted, I dozed off, only to be rudely awakened by a nurse who informed me that Henry's respiratory status was failing, even though he remained on the ventilator in the ICU.

By the time I arrived in the unit, the resident had already ordered a repeat chest X-ray, blood counts, full electrolyte panel, and arterial blood gases. "I need his volume status, and who is the lung doc on call?"

The trauma of Henry's multiple injuries were causing edema. Intravenous fluids had been poured in and his body was not able to handle it all. The chest x-ray confirmed his lungs were also filling with fluid. His blood pressure was dipping to 80/40 with a heart rate of 120 with frequent runs of irregular heartbeats indicating cardiac irritability. Sedated from anesthesia, he looked peaceful, but his prognosis was poor.

"Give him 80 mg. Lasix IV and have the pulmonologist check his vent settings." I knew the diuretic might not reverse the fluid in his lungs, but it was worth a shot.

Standing there watching him deteriorate, I was in agony. Never before had I cursed my medical impotence so much, for with all the modern advances in medicine, there was nothing more that I could do.

"Are there any further orders, Dr. Braddock?" The ICU nurse asked quietly.

I shook my head. "No. Just continue to monitor him and keep his IV fluids limited to 50 cc an hour."

The ICU was staffed by experts in the field and there really was no reason to stay and watch Henry, but my legs were leaden, and I could not tear my eyes away from his face. Did I have any gloating satisfaction that Arkady/Henry was getting his dues? No. I was trying my best to save him when I could have easily killed him. Fate stepped in now and all I could do was watch and hope that he would beat the odds and survive.

While standing over Henry in my anxiety, the cardiac monitor showed rapid ventricular tachycardia.

No... Damn it, NO! If I could reestablish his cardiac function there was still a chance to save him. I knew I was grasping at straws, but I wasn't going to just stand by and watch him die.

I went into action again. "Get the crash cart and prepare to defibrillate."

Nurses rushed in with the defibrillator and medications for more heroic measures. I could tell that both the resident on duty and the nurses were looking at me as if I had lost my mind, but none dared to contradict me.

Was I delaying the inevitable, torturing the man who was seriously injured before his final exit? "When there is life, there is hope." Who said that inane phrase? Henry was unconscious and didn't know what was being done to him. Or did he? Unconscious he might have been, but could he sense my presence?

I kept fighting for his life. The nurse fired up the defibrillator and gave him one shock which brought him back to a normal sinus rhythm. I ordered more IV medications to control his heart rhythm.

I stayed at the hospital all night, going in and out of the ICU, occasionally grabbing a cup of coffee and standing by the window to watch the stream of pedestrians going in and out of the hospital and cars slowly circling the parking lot looking for a vacant spot that wasn't there. Mundane, everyday life with its haste, frustrations, anxieties, fears and solace, grief and comfort was there before me. It kept me in the present. In the morning, when I went back to ICU, Henry opened his eyes and began coughing against the ventilator tube.

I took in a deep breath and exhaled slowly, watching Henry come back to life. The nurse on duty smiled at me and I smiled back. Then I patted Henry on the shoulder. "I know it's uncomfortable, chum, but bear with us a while longer. You scared the hell out of me, but you're on the mend now."

Henry blinked and frowned, then stared at me, and I knew he wanted to know what had happened to him. I described his injuries and what surgeries we had to do. I took his hand and assured him that there was no damage to his spine. I felt a slight squeeze of my hand and this small gesture meant more to me than any words he could have said.

After making sure he was made as comfortable as possible, I felt I could safely leave him in the care of the qualified staff and went home for a much needed rest.

* * *

I parked the car in the garage and walked into the house. Gretchen, who was sipping coffee in our breakfast room, slowly rose from her chair and stared at me with ill-concealed fear all over her face.

"He'll live," I said wearily, lowering myself into the chair.

Gretchen closed her eyes and with a deep sigh sank back into her chair.

"Henry will be O.K. As I told you on the phone, he had a ruptured spleen and a few fractures. It was touch and go for a while because he lost a lot of blood, but he'll make it. He's stable now."

I watched Gretchen's face carefully. After the initial relief on her face, I saw nothing but a mask of natural concern that anyone would have had for a friend.

She shook her head. "My God, that's terrible! I can see why you stayed with him all night. I hope he continues to improve. Since Tom Waverly didn't, you must be very anxious about Henry."

A vein started pulsating in my temple. With great difficulty I controlled my voice, "Tom Waverly is not the only patient I've lost in my career," I said carefully. "It doesn't make a damn bit of difference who the patient is. It's never easy to lose one." I plopped my briefcase on the kitchen tile counter a bit harder than I intended and it startled Gretchen.

"Why are you angry, Jim? I meant nothing by my remark."

"Then why use Tom Waverly's name?"

Gretchen shrugged. "It was the first name that came to mind."

"You didn't need to name anyone."

"Why are you so touchy, darling? I told you, I meant nothing by it."

"I just didn't like the implication, that's all."

"None was intended, Jim," Gretchen said quietly.

After a tough night, my nerves were on edge and I wanted to continue the argument, to put her on the defensive and play once again the role of a wronged husband.

I checked myself just in time. It took a supreme effort not to bring up the past and accuse her again of infidelity.

After several deep breaths, I controlled myself. "I guess I am really beat, Gretchen. Tough night. How about a cup of coffee?"

Gretchen gave me a long look. "Are you sure you wouldn't like to have some breakfast first? I can whip up an omelet or scrambled eggs and toast."

"Well, now that you mention it, I'd love some eggs." I forced a smile. "Thank you."

Gretchen got busy in the kitchen and while I waited, I sipped some hot coffee and tried to relax. In no time at all, I had my scrambled eggs and toast.

As I ate, I gave Gretchen all the details of what took place at the hospital.

She listened attentively, with loving sympathy on her face. When I finished, she said, "I think you went beyond the call of duty in trying to save him. All I can say, is that I am so very proud of you." She circled my neck with her arms and pressed her head to my chest. "I love you darling," she whispered and I held her close, too emotionally overcome to say anything.

*   *   *

Henry's recovery was rapid, considering the degree of trauma he had sustained. I checked on him every day while he was in the hospital and was pleased that there were no complications of any kind. In due time, he recovered completely and returned to work. His gratitude to me was deep and sincere, and over time as we often worked side-by-side, I came to appreciate his even temper, his good humor, his kindness to patients even under trying circumstances, and ever so gradually, I worked through my resentment of him and actually learned to like him.

At long last, early in June, Gretchen and I were able to go to Europe for a much needed vacation.

CHAPTER 15

When we arrived in Germany, Gretchen's mother was delighted to see us and as on our previous visits, offered a variety of coffee cakes and pastries along with chocolate bonbons and butter cookies. Dressed in a flowing dark green dress with a crocheted white collar, she had changed little except that her hair was almost white with only a few strands of brown mixed in. In addition to her hair, a few more wrinkles, and a few more pounds signified the passing of years. I watched with indulgence as Gretchen and Frau Schneider launched into an exchange of nonstop reminiscences, at times chuckling, at times serious. I could not keep up with their galloping German and was content to watch their animated faces.

We spent a few days in Frankfurt, and then with promises to return soon, we said goodbye to Frau Schneider and drove south to Heidelberg.

June in that picturesque city of The Student Prince, was sunny and fragrant with field flowers and blooming trees. We stayed at the Europa Hotel on *Anlage Strasse*, which was flanked by rows of chestnut trees that provided shade for leisurely strollers. By day we roamed the familiar streets, the echo of German flooding us with memories of our courtship. We retraced our steps of years before, drank beer and ate bratwurst with sauerkraut and pumpernickel bread at the *Roten*

Ochsen pub, dined at a variety of restaurants on the *Hauptstrasse,* climbed the hills to the burnt out castle, rode the excursion boat down the Neckar River as the accordionist played tunes from the Student Prince. Sentimental? Trite? Perhaps. But we loved it and felt as if twenty years had melted away and we were young again.

We drove on the other side of the Neckar to a neighboring village where I parked the car along the road and stole a couple of juicy apples from a roadside orchard with Gretchen nervously watching.

"What if the *polizei* drive past and arrest you?" she said shading her eyes from the sun and looking down the road.

"I'll tell them I heard that German apples are juicier than ours and I simply had to taste one."

"Sure. And if they hauled you into jail just the same? The local newspapers would have a field day. I can just see the headline: *Prominent American Surgeon Caught Stealing Apples... Arrested and taken to jail until further notice.*" Gretchen couldn't restrain herself any further and burst out laughing.

I shook my finger at her. "Your laugh always gets to me. You say another word and I'll silence you right there in the back seat of our car. Then what will the *polizei* say to the newspaper, hmm?"

Gretchen beckoned to me. I bit into one apple and handed her the other. I climbed behind the wheel and suddenly it became imperative for me to talk to her, to tell her of my love for her, so I drove back toward the hotel, although it was only early afternoon.

Surprised, Gretchen looked at me. "Don't you want to stop at a café for tea and cake? It's so early yet."

I shook my head and kept driving.

Our room was large and furnished in the Louis XVth style. The French doors opened onto a small balcony overlooking the *Anlage Strasse,* its chestnut trees restless in the afternoon breeze.

Tenderly I pulled her toward me. She gave in easily and pressed her face against my chest. "Oh, darling, I am so glad the past is over. We've learned a hard lesson." Her voice was muffled against my chest, but I felt her warm breath.

"Hon, this is all behind us. How about my calling down for a bottle of champagne?"

She smiled and lifted her face to me for a kiss. "A little later, perhaps?" she whispered, reaching for my shirt and unbuttoning it.

I was instantly aroused by the delicate touch of her fingernails gently scratching my bare chest. It felt as though I had never made love to her before, and I saw her in a new light, this lovely woman who not only had forgiven me, but confessed her own transgressions, this gentle yet strong woman who stood by me and loved me through two other lifetimes.

In silence we undressed each other, in reverence we touched each other, in wonder we discovered new meaning in the tender worship of our nakedness and the urgent joining of our bodies. In the soaring flight of mind as I drowned my senses in her, I heard her cry out in the perfect union of a man and a woman who had rediscovered each other at last.

As we lay in each other's arms, I turned her face toward me. "Gretchen, darling, I wish I had the right words to tell you how I love you, and how much your love means to me. I want to prove to you that I have changed. I feel as if I was reborn, a different man starting over in a new and wonderful life."

She put her hand over my mouth. "I know all this, Jim. I feel it and am deeply grateful for being given a second chance at happiness. You don't have to convince me. I can see it every day in everything you do and say. Your heart attack has taught me some things as well. I nearly lost you, but you survived and are well now, so we must treasure every day, every hour, every minute of our lives from now on."

She burrowed her face in the crook of my arm and we stayed that way for a while in contented silence.

*   *   *

In the ensuing days, we made love more often than in the last few years of our marriage and I was amused to think that the force of our passion was something I had always thought was reserved for the very young.

At the end of our stay, we visited Baden-Baden and watched the gamblers at the casino for a while. Men and women in their formal clothes saw their fortunes slip away before their eyes, and only an occasional fast-breathing matron scooped her winnings with her bejeweled hands. The smell of tobacco and strong perfume wafted toward us as we stood behind the players sitting around the table. No one spoke and only the croupier's monotonous voice cut through the silence, urging the gamblers to place their bets. Tension hung suspended in the atmosphere.

Without a word, I pulled Gretchen out of the casino and into the cool fresh air outside. She followed me eagerly and once outside, gave a quick shudder. "I could never become a gambler. What a horrible atmosphere! And more often than not a losing battle at the gaming table. What a way to throw away one's fortune. What a punishing addiction."

I nodded. "I can't imagine being drawn to the gaming table. The tension, the electricity around those gamblers... What an atmosphere in there!"

But outside, the gardens were rich with flowers lovingly cared for, and we walked hand-in-hand, pausing at each flower bed and sipping tea with cakes at the outdoor café. From there we went back to Frankfurt after deciding not to drive to Bavaria. We enjoyed our vacation but now were eager to get back home to Steve. We looked in on Gretchen's mother one more time and then caught the plane to San Francisco.

*   *   *

We returned home to find to our delight that Steve had been accepted at Stanford to start his art courses. It was our hope that after he graduated, he would be accepted to do his graduate work in graphic art.

I counted myself among the luckiest of men and felt that nothing could mar my happiness, for I knew that I had paid my dues and deserved the reprieve. My physical exam showed that I was in good shape and the only warning from the cardiologist was not to exert myself either physically or emotionally.

Refreshed from our trip, we reveled in rediscovering each other. That Steve had noticed our happiness was obvious from his lopsided, sly grin whenever he looked at us sitting close together on our couch in the family room, or holding hands for no reason at all.

"Hey, you guys, may I ask you a favor?" he once asked and when we nodded, he said, "Please cool it when I bring my friends over to the house." He winced a little, then covered up with a smile, "You know, you're my *parents* after all!"

We laughed and nothing more was said, but in private, Gretchen put her hand on my arm and said, "He's right, you know. Remember that I said this to you once before? We should not act like young newlyweds in his presence. It's embarrassing to him. Say what you may about the sophistication of modern youth, still, we are old folks in his mind. We shouldn't be holding hands, or hugging, or giving each other those suggestive looks."

I was taken aback. "My God, you're right. I haven't realized how it looked to our son." Then I added sheepishly, "Are we *that* obvious?"

Gretchen laughed. "I guess we are. I didn't realize it either. That makes two of us!"

I looked over my shoulder to make sure Steve was out of the room and then pulled Gretchen into my arms and whispered into her ear, "We'll have to sneak behind our son's back, then. Makes for more fun."

She went out of the room shaking her red hair off her forehead in a familiar gesture. I asked her once why she did it and her answer was to shrug and toss the words over her shoulder, "I don't know. Just feels good to do it." And that was that. For me, it signified the end of whatever discussion was taking place and a bit of feminine vanity to underscore the beauty and lushness of her hair.

Careful to follow my cardiologist's warning to slow down, I had placed myself on call every fourth weekend. It was quite a shock to realize that my colleagues managed quite well without my being there most of the time. Slightly chagrined at this puncture to my vanity, I nonetheless was able to laugh it off. Not so in the past. That was something else I noticed about myself -- I'd acquired a measure of humility and was able to laugh at myself, a newly discovered trait. What was the old saying? The king is dead, long live the king? And so it was with me. Well, not quite. I was still able to do surgery, see patients, take part in the residency teaching program and the most important of all, feel needed. So what if I was no longer running breathlessly down the hospital halls at every emergency call, and that I deferred the most difficult surgical procedures requiring long hours in the operating room to a younger colleague? My personal rewards far outweighed these professional concessions.

Now that Steve was about to graduate from high school and embark on college work, he and I grew closer and I was happy that he frequently came to me for advice.

One late morning as I was about to sit down with a book, he

entered the room and stood watching me for a few seconds, shuffling his feet. I closed the book. "Come in, Steve. Need some input?"

He walked in and sat in the chair opposite me. I studied him for a few seconds. I had forgotten how much he had grown in the last couple of years. Six foot three, a good three inches over me, red-haired like his mother with her light complexion, he inherited my dark brows and the result was that he was every high school girl's heart throb. I thanked my lucky stars that it didn't go to his head and he enjoyed their attention in a detached way, dating various girls often but not going steady with any of them. An amorous distraction could have brought his grades a notch down, just enough to make it difficult to be accepted by the university of his choice.

He looked relaxed now, dressed in faded blue jeans, gray T-shirt, and white socks and sneakers. He liked these shirts which he wore with shirttails over his jeans – the sloppy style I disliked. His hair was longer than I would have liked to see him wear, but it did not come down to his shoulders and for that I was grateful. Thanks for little favors as the old cliché goes.

"Dad, could we talk a bit about the units I'll be taking in my freshman year?" he asked looking at me with eagerness.

"Of course, Steve. You know how interested I am in everything you do. I'll be glad to give any advice I can."

"Thanks, Dad." He then proceeded to place before me the neatly typed subjects he needed to take and those he would like to add.

We spent a good part of an hour talking back and forth, lining up various possibilities. I strongly advised him to broaden his curriculum.

"Be aware, Steve," I went on, "that any courses heavy on art alone are limiting. Include subjects unrelated to it. In order to be a well-rounded person, you need a broader education. Think about it and let me know what you decide."

"I know, Dad," Steve said with an impish grin, "I already thought of anthropology as my minor."

"Good idea. I'm proud of you, son. Sign up for it."

I was pleased by his initiative, but I had something else on my mind.

"There's something else," I went on. "Do listen to your teacher's point of view as well."

"That depends upon the teacher, Dad. I listen, but I don't always agree."

The boy has a mind of his own. I was impressed. "So, you are discerning, Steve. That's good! And I didn't mean that you must take the teacher's word as gospel, only that it may give you a broader perspective on the subject discussed."

Steve smiled and rose to leave. "I've got to go, Dad. Thanks for the tip."

I rose too and hesitantly reached out to hug him but then dropped it. We were never a hugging and kissing family and now I regretted it. Steve saw my gesture and with one arm holding his note book, he unabashedly hugged me with another. "See ya, Dad," he said and strolled out of the room.

I swallowed hard and blinked several times to clear the moisture that suddenly clouded my sight. I strolled back to my chair near the window overlooking our garden and swimming pool and picked up my book. But it sat on my lap unopened as I looked out on our flowerbeds. I so enjoyed puttering in the garden and I could see the results of my care. The geraniums were nurtured, faded blooms carefully picked, as were a half a dozen rose bushes thoughtfully planted to mix the red, yellow and salmon pink varieties. Suddenly I thought of the roses I had seen in Dr. Farnsworth's garden and the memory gave me a jolt. No matter how carefully I tended to ours, the result was a pale simile to the brilliance of the other world's colors.

With a concerted effort I chased away the unexpected intrusion and focused again on the garden. It was *our* garden, planted with my own hands, and here, tangible, fragrant, accessible to us as a family. Many happy hours were to be spent here from now on with many exciting events to experience, Steve's high school graduation, his entrance to the college of his choice, his future graduation from college and then, with luck, graduate work in graphic art. I felt my chest swell with pride at a very human satisfaction that my only son, my only child, chose a profession with wide possibilities for his future. A twinge of disappointment, however, dampened it a little. My dream of having my son follow in my footsteps and become a physician had been dashed. I aborted the dangerous thought before I allowed it to fester. Old habits die hard, I thought, but at least I was able to control them now.

Gretchen and I were going to build a new life for ourselves. A life centered on our small family, the closeness of our relationship, late as it had come, but even more precious now. All the trauma of the past years was of my own doing of course, and how fortunate it turned out for me to have been able to see the folly of my previous years and be forever grateful for a second chance at life and happiness.

I realized suddenly that I had never thanked Dr. Farnsworth for all he had done for me, but somehow I knew that he was aware of my gratitude. I turned my thoughts to other things. In a few weeks Steve would graduate and Gretchen and I would be sitting among other proud parents watching our child in cap and gown receive his first diploma on the long road to his coveted graduate work. Each step would be a progressively greater joy for us to experience.

I glanced at my watch. It was noon. A long afternoon stretched before me. I shifted in my chair. Restlessness wormed itself into my mind and with it a clear picture of the young woman with a breast lump that I had operated on the day before. It seemed like a benign tumor until I opened her up and sent the lump to the pathologist for a quick diagnosis. It turned out to be one of the more virulent breast cancers. I did a lumpectomy and took out a good number of lymph nodes to see if the cancer had already spread.

It would be a kindness on my part, even though I was off duty this weekend, to drop in on her and give her what comfort I could under the circumstances.

"What are you plans for this afternoon, Gretchen?" I called to her from the family room. In a few moments, she came in from the kitchen. Dressed in faded blue jeans and a matching vest over a white cotton shirt, she looked like a teenager. She wiped her hands on her apron looking somewhat guilty. "I thought since you are so comfortably settled with a book here, and probably need a nap later, I would call one of my friends and we'd go do some shopping. They have advertised some good sales and you know me and sales!" She smiled sheepishly and looked to me for comment.

"Hon, you go ahead. Before I have that nap you're talking about, I thought I'd run back to the hospital and check on the woman I operated on yesterday for breast cancer."

Before Gretchen could protest, I raised my hand. "Don't worry, I promise to make this just a charitable call without involving myself in further care. I won't be long and by the time you come home from your shopping, I'll be sitting right here with this book." I lifted it in the air and smiled.

As she left to fix us a sandwich for lunch, I settled back in my chair and opened the book, listening to the homey sounds from the kitchen: Gretchen opening the refrigerator, taking out dishes from the cabinet, the rustling of a paper bag in the bread bin. I stared at the pages without reading them. Then slowly, I put down the book on the coffee table and walked into the kitchen.

She had the bread board hooked over the sink and a sourdough loaf on it. I took the knife out of her hand and started slicing the loaf. As I cut into it, the soft, fresh bread collapsed.

Gretchen laughed. "Honey, you're pressing on the bread. You have to saw it. Here, let me show you."

I watched her and then tried it myself. It worked, except the slices were uneven and on a bias. I lay the knife on the board, spread my arms in a helpless gesture, and started opening the cold cuts. When I turned toward Gretchen, she was standing still, watching me. Our glances locked.

Her eyes reddened and there were tears in them. "You've never... In the kitchen... Such a small thing... I mean together, we..." her voice broke and she busied herself over the sandwiches. I pulled her toward me and kissed her on the forehead. I knew exactly what she meant. I was always too busy to share in domestic chores, the little things that draw couples together, and the comfort of silent, shared habits.

Little pleasures of life. How did I miss them all these years?

After lunch, we kissed each other and went our separate ways. I didn't bother putting on a coat and tie to go to the hospital and went out dressed as I was in a beige turtleneck and brown denim slacks. Another concession to my newly acquired leisurely dress code when I was off duty. I called goodbye to Gretchen who was still in the bedroom changing clothes, and grabbing a windbreaker, wallet and car keys, walked out of the house.

As I drove out of the garage, I decided that on the way back from the hospital I would stop at a florist and surprise Gretchen with a dozen red roses for no reason at all except to remind her that I loved her. My only regret was that nearly half of our life was already gone. How I wished that I had my life to live over differently. But there were many years ahead to make up to Gretchen, and because I rediscovered my love for her, those would be rewarding and happy years.

*   *   *

My patient, Anne Goodman, was awake and reasonably pain-free with the help of medication. She gave me a weak smile when I walked into her room and sat down by her bed.

"Dr. Braddock...how glad...to see you...so many questions...I need answers..." her voice was tremulous and weak, but her obvious relief upon seeing me was a gratifying proof that I was right in coming over to see her.

I patted her hand. "Take it easy, Anne. I'll stay as long as you like, just don't strain or hurry with your questions. Let me first tell you what we found. It was a very small lump which turned out to be malignant. I took it out together with a good number of lymph nodes to be on the safe side, but because the tumor was so small, I doubt that it has spread. I expect an excellent recovery."

She turned her head away from me. "And what if the lymph nodes are involved?"

I took her hand in mine and squeezed it. "There are a number of options, Anne. Several types of chemotherapy, drugs, radiation, etc. all should have good results with such a small tumor as yours. But as I said, I doubt that in your case any lymph nodes would be involved."

When she turned her head toward me, tears ran down the side of her face onto the pillow. "I am only thirty-four years old, Dr. Braddock. I have a wonderful husband and three young children. I hope you're right!" The last phrase was a wrenching cry from the soul even though her voice was weak and hoarse.

I tried to reassure her the best I could and she finally fell silent when she could no longer find a reason to say "Yes, but..." I rose to leave, knowing full well that she did not believe me and would not get rid of that insidious seed of doubt planted in her by the raw fact that she had cancer. I felt like a hypocrite giving her a rosy hope for recovery, fully aware that with the virulent type of cancer that she had, her full recovery was doubtful at best. I often wondered how oncologists cope with their daily cancer patients, so many of whom sooner or later, lose their battle with this dreaded disease. Selfishly, I couldn't help but be thankful again for the happiness I was enjoying and the future that loomed so bright.

On the way back I stopped to buy roses for Gretchen, but could not get Anne out of my mind. The greatest frustration of all was to hold back what I would have liked to tell her, to share my knowledge of the other side of life, how little there was to be afraid of, and how beautiful it was. I wanted to tell her that her children would still have their father and grandparents, if indeed the cancer should eventually kill her, and that she would not really be dead, but very much alive and well on the other side of life.

And as I drove home, I thought of how lucky I really was, for on both sides of life I had love -- Gretchen/Irene in this life, and Nadine/Louise in the other.

After crossing the Golden Gate Bridge, the majesty of its span dwarfing me, I glanced over San Francisco Bay with its blue waters sparkling in the sun, dozens of sailboats straining against the fresh breeze funneling from the ocean. On the other side, I looked up at the hills of Marin lush with oak, eucalyptus, buckeye, liquidambar, yellow broom, all glowing in the rays of the sun and sharing space with an eclectic variety of homes. Never had the scene appeared more beautiful or more alive to me. I reached for the roses and inhaled their fragrance. I could see Gretchen in the kitchen arranging them in her favorite crystal vase and fussing over each stem. I laughed softly in anticipation of watching her delight.

As I emerged from the tunnel and coasted down a hill, a sudden crushing pain in my chest sliced through my laughter. Like a stomping foot of an elephant it pressed, spreading the pain into my left arm, bathing me in cold sweat. I clutched the wheel tightly, pulled off on the shoulder and turned on the emergency flashing lights. I fumbled for the phone, but the sky, the clouds, the trees and the hills swirled in a kaleidoscope of color and brilliant sparks. Then the world around me began to darken, and this time I knew what the pain would do.

CHAPTER 16

Fifteen years later

S teve's hands are shaking so violently that further typing is impossible. He pushes his chair away from the table and begins to pace the floor of his study. Weekends have become a nightmare. He knows that Jean resents his shutting himself up in the den and coming out hours later tense, bewildered, and frequently distraught.

After four years of marriage and two miscarriages, her pregnancy now is drawing to an end and she needs his help around the house. But today especially, Steve cannot leave the den. He is held captive by an invisible presence, a presence so powerful, so familiar, and so insistent that he succumbs readily to its influence. Yes. His father's influence. It has been building up over the last year. Steve senses his father's presence. It has happened before, at the funeral, at the door to his mother's bedroom, and in that dream as if it had not been a dream at all but a true, real-life visit. It had first happened a day after the fatal heart attack when Steve suddenly awakened in the middle of the night and half-asleep, half-awake saw a shadow by the side of his bed, the unmistakable head of hair and profile, as his father bent over him and kissed him on the cheek.

Shaken, grieving, Steve said nothing about it to his mother and after the funeral he hovered over her, trying hard to alleviate her numbing grief by spending as much time with her as his studies for high school finals permitted.

Gretchen alternated between copious tears and cold, zombie-like behavior, walking around the house from room to room and muttering to Steve, "I can't understand why it happened. They told me he recovered so well. Jim was good about working less... exercising... I can't understand... he seemed so well..." Over and over she voiced her anguish until Steve ran out of consoling words and decided to call Henry Manchester to come over and talk to Gretchen.

While Jim was still alive, Henry had visited them often, always bringing gifts -- A bottle of *Veuve Clicquot,* or an elaborate plant for the patio, or a bottle of fine brandy. Invariably he told Jim that he could never repay him for saving his life. Jim admonished him for his extravagances and finally told him that while he was welcome to visit, he was embarrassing him with his profuse gratitude.

When Steve called Henry, he readily agreed to come and arrived with a bouquet of spring flowers. He talked to Gretchen for an hour while Steve discreetly went to his room. For one so young, he had sensed that Henry was the right person to calm Gretchen. And so he did. After he left, Gretchen hugged Steve. "Darling, I promise that I'll try to cope better from now on. It's been hard on you too. I've been selfish. I know Dad wouldn't want me to go to pieces."

Gradually, Gretchen took hold of herself and glowed with pride at Steve's graduation.

He plunged into his college studies determined to do well in art and anthropology. But after a few months, he became bored with his studies and decided to go back to medicine. As the years went by however, it became amply evident that he was not cut out to be a surgeon. Clumsy with his hands, hating the operating room, he finally had to concede that his original thought of becoming a cardiologist was the right way to go. For years he felt that he had failed his father and wished that somehow Jim would give him some sign of approval.

As it turned out, he was able to devote himself entirely to his studies without worrying about his mother. A few months after his father died, Henry Manchester showed up at the house again, this time bearing a dozen red roses. His visits became regular, and it wasn't long before Steve realized that the relationship between his mother and Henry had become serious. A year after Jim died Gretchen told Steve that she and Henry were going to be married. Steve was delighted. He liked Henry very much and was happy to see his mother work through her grief and regain her happy disposition.

After his own marriage to Jean, a registered nurse whom he met while doing his residency training, Gretchen and Henry bought a condominium and Steve and Jean moved into the house.

About a year ago, Steve overheard a friend speak of automatic writing as the simplest way to communicate with the dead. Intrigued, he had gone to the library and read on the subject. It sounded easy. No joining of hands, no darkened rooms, no witnesses.

One morning he asked Jean not to disturb him and went into his den to try an experiment. He spent a few minutes meditating, then sat down at his computer, closed his eyes, said a prayer, and emptying out his mind, placed his fingers on the keyboard.

He had read that he could not expect definite results from the start, nevertheless, when words started to enter his mind and he put them on paper without stopping to analyze what he was typing, excitement mounted within him. For a few days he systematically repeated the procedure and the messages that came through began to have coherence and continuity of thought. Fragments of philosophy, abstract and esoteric, they were definitely nothing that he himself would have written.

Then one day, as he placed his fingers on the keyboard again, words and phrases tumbled through that were unmistakably his father's. Reminiscences and accurate, humorous incidents from his childhood that only his father could have known were obviously intended to leave no doubt as to who was dictating.

One of the first things that came through was his father's comment on Steve's failure to follow in his father's footsteps. "You made a smart decision, son," he dictated. "Not everyone is cut out to be a surgeon. It's a mistake to choose a specialty you're not comfortable with. I'm pleased as it is that you've gone back to medicine after all. I went along with your wish to try graphic art, but needless to say, I was delighted to see you so successful in cardiology."

From that day on, Steve has been writing down everything that has come through. He can no more stop these sessions before his father has finished the story of his other side of life than he can make Jean understand his craving to know of his father's life after death.

Today's session however, is too much. It is difficult for him to relive the day of his father's death fifteen years ago when he came home to find his mother sobbing in the living room, a dozen wilted roses in her lap. Yet he senses his father's need to describe his side of life and to help Steve understand his parents' marital problems. Now that he knows, Steve can forgive his father and thus lift the burden that both of them had carried since his death. Although his mother grieved for a long time, she is now happy with Henry who has given her a second chance at happiness, and Steve is glad that he and Jean had moved into the house before the child is born.

Still in his den, restless, Steve looks out the window. The sun is sparkling on the immaculate golf course that spreads before him like a vast, plush carpet. It is only eight o'clock in the morning but already golfers are rolling down the slopes in their golf carts dotting the fairway like scattered ladybugs on a verdant canvas. He is glad that he has moved the study into the guest room where the view is spectacular.

Ordinarily, when the flow of dictation ceased or became unintelligible, he knew it was time to stop for the day. He often wondered whether after a particularly long session his own mind would wander off and admit nonsense from the world of shadows, or his father's mental transmitter would weaken and then drift off. Jim has told him much about the other side of his existence and the fact that he has been reunited with his love from another life. It took Steve a while to assimilate everything that his father has told him, but the most important thing was to know that his father was happy.

This morning however, the atmosphere in his study is charged with tension. He eyes the keyboard with reluctance yet senses that something out of the ordinary is about to happen. Some urgency, relentless, unspoken, holds him in the room. Fighting his desire to leave, Steve goes back to the computer. Almost immediately his father begins to dictate.

"Steve, I'm glad you picked up my message again. I've been trying to get you to have one more session this morning. What a different perspective one has on this side! It's painful to relive episodes from your lives, the ones that the conscious mind conveniently blots out from memory. To see where you have erred and to be impotent to undo the harm – that's the true hell of belated remorse.

"And this brings me to what I need to tell you. I've sensed for quite some time that you've been spending more and more time at the hospital or poring over journals at home. Remember what I've told you about my relationship with your mother and how I took my marriage for granted? Your profession is important but not to the exclusion of everything else. You need to spend more time with Jean. Don't ignore her. Don't repeat my mistake."

Steve stops typing and sits staring at the computer screen. His father's admonition makes him squirm in his seat. Over the last few months Jean has been complaining about his absences and lack of attention to what she was saying when he was home. He has brushed her off each time with some lame excuse or other. Steve shifts in his seat. The memory of his parents' estrangement has hit home. He's been a blind fool to allow the pattern to start repeating itself in his own marriage.

He places his hands on the keyboard again.

"I see that my message has gotten through, son. I'm glad. As for me, Nadine has given me not only great new happiness but moral support as well. Yet, I have the feeling that I am to move on to another place. I've talked to Dr. Farnsworth about what I've done over here to make up for some of my past and I have a feeling this might be our last communication for quite some time. It is difficult, if not impossible, to explain how this certainty comes to me. It's more than a feeling – a kind of recognition of a change that is about to occur. There's no ambivalence, no doubt. Just the certainty. I felt it as I was talking to the professor a little while ago and although he has not said it in so many words, I know that my stay here is coming to an end. Oh, Steve, there was so much more I was going to tell you. Are you still with me, I wonder? All the errors I perpetrated – they were sins of omission mostly. I am rambling again. I do hope you are getting all this.

"Strange animals we humans are. We fight, we compete, we strive for independence yet we detest isolation. We fear loneliness. Although I am looking for a change, yet I'm apprehensive. Perhaps I shall be able to make peace with my past and enter that state of rest that I have yearned for ever since making this transition.

"I'm excited, Steve. Can you understand that? Call it anticipation of a new adventure, the thrill of the unknown, I don't know. I feel much like a little kid who's been promised a great holiday but doesn't know where he is going and is afraid of being lost. Don't misunderstand me when I talk about remorse for past failures. That's the emotional torture of our own making and has nothing to do with the place I've been in over here. It's beautiful beyond earthly comprehension. There simply aren't any words to describe the brilliance of colors, the crystalline air, the perpetual freshness of nature, and the glorious sounds of music.

"Nevertheless, I am restless now and look forward to whatever is in store for me. Don't ask how I know. I can't answer that. I just do.

"I think I'm going to leave now, Steve.

"Steve! Are you there?...Can you hear...."

*   *   *

Stunned, Steve sits motionless in front of the computer and waits for further words. None come. Why was his father's communication cut off in mid-sentence? Steve tries to blank out his mind but no message comes through. Silence settles in his brain. Crawls into the room. Permeates it.

He listens. He hopes to hear more. Nothing. Somehow he has lost contact with his father and with a sinking feeling is convinced that it is permanent.

Then a pulse begins to throb in his temples. Alert, tense, he listens now to the sounds in the house.

There is an urgent knock on the door which echoes, pounds in Steve's eardrums. And words. They reach his brain and enthrall him. Jean's words.

"Steve! Come quick! I'm in labor!"

*   *   *

In the hospital, Steve paces the floor outside the delivery room, wondering whether it will be a boy or a girl. They decided not to find out the sex of the baby ahead of time, and be surprised. He and Jean have agreed a long time ago, that if the child is a boy, they would call him Jim.

The baby, healthy and vocal, is indeed a boy, and soon Steve is allowed to hold him. Tears well in his eyes as he looks into the baby's face, then bends over, kisses the tiny fist and whispers,

"Hello, Jim!"